Best,

Camden Joy

Pan

Pan

A WORK OF IMAGINATION ENDEAVORING TO RECOUNT
THE EXTRAORDINARY YET TRUE EVENTS OCCURRING
WITHIN THE CITY OF NEW YORK UPON APRIL THE
SEVENTH, NINETEEN HUNDRED AND NINETY-EIGHT
WHEN: NUMEROUS HEARTS ARE ENGAGED: FEATS OF
ASTONISHMENT AND DARING UNFOLD: A MAN LOSES
HIS FOUND LOVE: A PRIMITIVE POWER DRAWS
MANIFOLD STRANGERS INTO A SUPERNATURAL
DRAGNET: A FATHER'S GIFT SENDS A SON ACROSS THE
OCEAN: SPACE-TIME CONTINUUMS (QSTs) ARE
REPEATEDLY STRADDLED: TEARS GET SHED: AFTER
WHICH THE ASSEMBLAGE OF CROSS ENTERTAINERS
KNOWN AS THE FALL CEASES WORKING TOGETHER
(YET AGAIN) AND EVERYTHING THREATENS TO REMAIN
EXACTLY AS IT HAS BEEN DESPITE:

THE GENUINE ADVENTURES
FICTIONALIZED HEREWITH

a novella by

CAMDEN JOY AND COLIN B MORTON

Highwater Books

All contents © 2001 Camden Joy and Colin B Morton
First Printing: November 2001
ISBN: 0-9700858-7-7
10 9 8 7 6 5 4 3 2 1

End note No. 2 was previously published in *Puncture #40*.

Published by Highwater Books
P.O. Box 1956
Cambridge MA 02238
(617) 628-2583
www.highwaterbooks.com

Publisher: Tom Devlin

Printed in Canada

...thus it passed, the Goat-beast son of Hermes by Penelope came caught in a trap set for stray flock. Bound by strongest cabling to three sleek horses, this One with the ears of a goat, and legs likewise, was hauled roaring before chieftains of the Celtae. They made it plain He who was thus tied was the Great One making men, like cattle, stampede. As the god of panic, honored by enemies as "Faunus" or "Pan," He was then sacrificed through stones and flame upon a pyre. The Celtae-chieftains had the Great One's Head buried without monument while the rest, His Body, was dispatched with men from the North, sea-dwellers of floating vessels. The sun blazed bright upon shields and helmets as this, the tribe of sailors, braved crashing foam of silver-blue sea to plant His Remains at the ends of the earth. Their noble journey was the wish of the chieftains, that never the powers of Pan could be restored. Though Pan were halved in such gruesome a manner, His Head, kept by the Celtae in the ground, occasioned sorcery to render the grave hot as the fires a warrior finds in beastly dens...

Accounts of the Western Peoples
AS RECORDED BY MAGNUS THE GOOD,
TR. BY R. TOTALE, 2 VOLS., 1923

THAT MORNING AT WORK, Clarke's secretary ushered two men into his office.

"Mr Clarke! I am glad to meet you."

"Good of you to spare the time."

"On such short notice."

"On such a day."

"Hopper," said the one.

"Fredericks," said the other.

They both stuck out their hands. The visitors wore slacks, sweater vests, dress shirts, all constructed out of an unusual reflective fabric that rustled like crepe paper. Clarke thought they behaved a bit like private investigators. Then again, what did he know of private investigators? He'd seen a few on television. He shook their hands.

"What can I do for you gentlemen?"

Hopper had an athletic build. He couldn't keep still. Fredericks had a head of light-brown hair blown straight back, making it look as if he'd ridden a roller coaster on the way over. They performed a choreographed reach for their wallets and displayed badges of some sort.

Clarke stood before his desk, arms crossed.

"You're welcome, of course. Please, have a seat. Can I offer you something to drink? Soda, juice, coffee, anything?"

"Water," Hopper agreed, "would be fine."

Clarke leaned backward to depress a button on the phone. His psychedelic necktie tickled the top of the promotional frog on his desk. That damn frog. The promotion had failed. The CD had absolutely tanked. Without a doubt, the frog would fetch more now than the CD. "Alice, one water and… " Clarke pointed at Fredericks, who shook his head. "Just one water, Alice. I'm good for coffee."

"We won't take up a lot of your time," Fredericks said, in a bored tone.

Hopper nodded. "Just here with a warning."

His secretary entered with a plastic glass of ice water and stepped out again.

Clarke's stomach rumbled. "A warning about what?"

"Oh, a little warning about…—Say, you've got a *very* nice office here." Hopper motioned at the tall windows, high ceiling, the elegantly spare furnishings. "What is this, six by ten meters?"

"It could be, at that." Clarke shrugged. "I'm not really very—"

"And a nice view." Fredericks whistled admiringly at the window.

"Of what, the Seagram Building?"

"Yes."

"Mmmm." It had never been one of Clarke's favorites.

"It's a Mies van der Rohe classic." Fredericks glowered at him. "A treasure."

"Oh."

"A landmark."

"Look, how can I... what can I do for you? I'm a little — "

Fredericks leaned forward, thrusting a photograph. He moved with such aggression, so swiftly, it concerned Clarke. "Do you recognize this man?"

Clarke took the picture with him behind his desk and sat down. He experienced a terrible sensation of sinking. He felt abruptly exhausted, unbearably so, like a man who had been out all night dancing at an after-hours club down in the sleaziest of quarters, swallowing gray energy caplets that came discreetly available at half past midnight, evaluating electronic cuts for the label, joshing with Jeremy and the rest about Brandon's latest health kick, cabbing home sweaty at five a.m., valiant and capable, the music still going 'round his head, youthfully certain that he had accomplished something important, this brave staying up late while others slept in their safe beds, this getting plugged in while cowards remained home. He was part of the revolution, if you believed the advertisements.

Clarke slowly nodded. "It's my friend Vaughn.

He's got this very distinctive mole on his forehead. He's standing in, well, it looks like Tompkins Square Park, you can see Charlie Parker's house in the back—"

"The man in the photo," Fredericks clarified, entering information in a miniature apparatus, "he's your friend?"

"Yeah."

"Vaughn?"

"Yeah."

Which reminds me, Clarke mused. *I have to give Vaughn a ring, let him know I'm still alive.* Vaughn had telephoned a couple times over the last several months and always Clarke was busy with this or that music convention. Well, a lot of being incessantly busy was just what it was like to be in A&R, it was a difficult job. Sometimes being a responsible employee meant being a bit of an irresponsible friend. For even when not being forced by Brandon to go chat up some hot young turntablist in London or Detroit or Amsterdam, Clarke had been obligated to attend some showcase of a still newer underground genius of breakbeats. And now, with the Seagram's deal pending, who knew what Clarke's new responsibilities would entail?

The two visitors exchanged the briefest of glances. Hopper scratched at his beard for a few moments then spoke. "That's what we were afraid of."

Fredericks was more blunt. "It can't continue, sir."

"We have been observing this Vaughn for…" Hopper gave it some thought, itched his scruffy beard again. "Well, for some time."

"We must ask that this friendship be surrendered."

This confused Clarke. "Is Vaughn in some kind of trouble?" That's the way it was always put in private investigator television shows, "some kind of trouble." That meant a misunderstanding, sometimes a misdemeanor, on rare occasion a felony.

"It's not what he is now. It's what he will become."

"The way we're putting it to you is this," Hopper spoke with grim regret. "You and this Vaughn can't be friends any longer."

Clarke smiled, for surely this was meant to be amusing.

Fredericks smiled back, but it chilled the spine. "We can't permit it to happen, sir."

Clarke wasn't sure what to say. This was some sort of prank, that much was clear. A test. Men showing up out of nowhere to declare such things. He thought to inquire if this were some sort of modern art pseudo-reality trip. Vaughn was probably earning college credit for this prank. But if it were a prank, would they admit it? That might forfeit the project's integrity. Clarke had read about rather highly regarded performance pieces involving surveillance, credit card calls, postal crimes, vanishings, cars left idling at the ends of driveways with their doors open, their drivers taken at gunpoint to storage lockers, demands posted on light poles in mall parking lots, the elements meticulously videotaped and later surfacing to great acclaim from art-house patrons and the like.

Fredericks shook his head sorrowfully. "This is no joke, sir."

"Well, it has to be. You are joking. Of course you are." Clarke hated how shrill his voice sounded. "You must be. Who ever heard of such a thing? It's like, I'm a child, and here comes my mother to tell me not to play with someone. Well, I'll tell you, you friend police! I... I..."

Hopper raised his eyebrows. "Yes?"

Clarke swooned, steadied himself.

"Oh, you're very tough." Fredericks sounded bored again. "Show him the rest of the pictures."

Clarke experienced a trace of sudden curiosity. More pictures! What would they show him? Then, just as quickly, his curiosity curdled into nausea. He realized he didn't want to know. His belly spasmed. He didn't want to hear himself let out a disgusted whimper, a moan. They had only been friends a few years. There was a lot about Vaughn about which he had no idea. He preferred it that way.

"Do I have to?" Hopper now had an imposing, dark envelope in his lap.

Yes, Clarke thought. *Does he have to?*

"He thinks Vaughn is a friend, you have to show him the pictures. That's procedure, remember? He has to learn what sort of operation he's involving himself with, what this friend is really like."

Clarke measured out a moment to consider what these men were saying. What made life so difficult? You fall for a girl, give her the world, she drops you like a safe from a bank window. You make it to Europe, spend your every cent to sleep with a dawn view of the harbor, and the jackhammers below the balcony immediately start up and never cease. You discard one rule after another, try to live by this or that guidebook, you get the taxi cab drivers who're new to the city, they drive with maps in their laps and cost you a fortune, or you don't see, until you're home, that your new market items appear to have been tampered with. The gas repairman arrives but ruins your plumbing. The plumber comes but ruins your electricity. The electrician comes but afterward nothing works right. The easy things are never easy. So much of our lives spent working backward on ourselves, regretting, fixing miscalculations. You dig up an inner resilience, continue to seek the new, to stay young even as your many college friends surrender to marriage, offspring, houses, suburbs, tedium, and one night buying a slice of pizza in a weak drizzle on the Lower East Side you happen upon a swell guy apparently down on his luck and you do him a favor, buy him a cream soda, hear his story, even ask his advice on your own things, you connect, it's a reassuring moment; you attend some shows, some flicks together, it's fun; then a year later, two men come from nowhere to tell you your new friend must be abandoned. Can such things be done? Who runs this place? Where do they keep the guidebooks?

Hopper scratched at his scruff some more, apologized to Clarke. Fredericks, though yawning, added his own regrets. "Neither of us likes this business, it's sickening, I honestly become sick over it. But it must get resolved."

Clarke swallowed. "I understand." But he understood none of it.

Hopper tapped the envelope to straighten the photos. He stood and brought them across the office, placed them on Clarke's desk.

Without warning, a side door flew open. All three men leapt in surprise. Music poured through, loud crashing drums and synthesizers. In strode a little, balding man clad in an oversized camouflage jumpsuit. It was the boss, Brandon, accessorized in his usual absurd sunglasses and elastic headband. "Clarke! I've got it, I've got it!" Brandon waved as if clearing away smoke. "Oh, I didn't realize you were in with some fuckheads."

Brandon half-turned to Fredericks and Hopper. "I mean, would you excuse us a moment; it'll be just a bit; make yourselves comfortable; your interest is extremely important to us; we'll be right back with you; fuck off and die; et cetera, et cetera."

Fredericks nodded. "It's okay."

"The Fall!" Brandon shouted at Clarke from a short distance. "Clarke, hey! The Fall; tonight at Brownie's; you remember, punk rockers from England? God, Clarke; fuck I always hated all those guitars; no more; The Fall's in town!"

Hopper snatched up the manila folder. "We'll come back later," he assured Clarke. He waved for Fredericks to follow him.

Brandon eyed them as the two men swept rapidly from Clarke's office. "Who're those fuckheads? Private dicks?"

"I... Maybe, I maybe think so."

"Oh well, whatever—The Fall! Turns out it's still alive but now it's techno; same singer, if you want to call that singing." Brandon shoved Clarke toward the side door. "Here, come with me; listen to this, these sounds, it's like... it's like... Hey! Anti-music!"

MEANWHILE, IN A FAR-OFF PLACE called Newport, Wales, the bell of a record shop rang and Colin B Morton entered. Sweet Alicia had her back to him while she used the computer behind the counter. Colin was gratified to meet her eyes as, reflected in the monitor, they swiveled to watch him. Alicia was dark-haired and pretty, with a pale complexion and a lanky body. Over the years, Colin had grown to adore her every flaw. The bad teeth. The insubstantial rump. The bored, awkward stances. Even the indie wuss trousers.

As for Colin, he was enormously handsome, with a glimmer of every brooding cinema star within him. Year after year, he was picked by *People* magazine second only to singer Tom Jones (nobody beats The King) as "Sexiest Welshman Alive."

"Darling girl," he called over to Sweet Alicia, "I'm off to the good ol' us of a this evening."

"Oh?" Alicia turned from the computer, and a smile like a butterfly flitted over her face. "Why's that?"

"Well, the head of Pan instructed me to."

"Wait." Alicia was floored. "You got yourself a Great God?"

From deep inside his dufflecoat, Colin extracted something like the horned skull of a faun or a satyr. He thunked it down on the glass-top counter. "Yeah. My dad was that guy in charge of the dig over in Caerleon," he explained. "And he turned over most everything they found, but for this. You'd like my dad. Last birthday, he sits me down in the kitchen and passes this over. 'Here's the head of Pan, son. Don't let no grubby sod from another continuum near it,' he tells me. 'That's right important. Just do whatever it commands you to do.—And listen, my boy: tidy your room once in a while.'"

"Oh," Sweet Alicia patted his arm sympathetically. "I know how it is. My dad gave me the Necronicom."

"Neat! Like that what Aleister Crowley had?"

Alicia flung around her sweet hair angrily. "John, piss on you, Jack! Aleister Crowley was just a guy with a creepy suit who couldn't count properly. No. Mine's the *original* Necronicom: ancient grimoire laden with energies of yore, the ownership of which endows enormous power but, y'know, ultimately leads to misfortune."

"Oh. I heard Jon Langford's brother wrote bits of it."

"Whatever. It was that one what Hitler had."

"How'd you get it?"

"Oh, same sort of affair," revealed Alicia. "Dad knocks at my bedroom the other month. 'Listen now,' he says, a bit bashful, and hands me this Necronicom. 'Book of dark lore for you, and turn that bloody music down.' Dad was born on the seventh hour of the seventh day of the seventh month, so he's often doing stuff like this. Dying and coming back to life, leaving his body, having fishes rain on him. Blah blah blah." Alicia fell silent, fidgeting absently with the vase of wilting daffodils next to the register. "How you gonna pay for the trip?"

"Oh, Pan told me to play the fruit machine at the pub."

"Ah, no fair! It's not gambling if Pan tells you when to play the slots. My, you're lucky. The Necronicom is bloody lame."

"Patience, my sweet. My head has been bloody worthless until now."

"So, you going to Las Vegas with Pan?"

"No. New York City. Where, if I understand correctly, I'm to see a musical rock group called The Fall. It's at the finish of a US tour, I 'spect."

"Oh." Alicia wasn't familiar with The Fall. She played bass in an indie wuss band, that cowardly pap flogged to kids. Colin, naturally, forgave every note for which she was responsible. "What are this Fall like?" she asked. "All's I know is that smelly nutters and dysfunctional kids what got no friends are the ones buying Fall records."

"Well, The Fall... It's definitely on the off-beaten path. It's not really like anything else, it's a bit... Hmm..." Colin stopped. Sweet Alicia still waited. "It's not," Colin said, with a chuckle, "as good as it used to be." This amused Colin, for it was the cry of every Fall fan down the ages. At any given moment, The Fall was not as good as it used to be. Initially, Colin explained, only he and Noj and Catherine and Sorry Ken had liked it, back at

Newport Stow Away. "They look like they've been let out of somewhere," a person in the crowd was heard to remark, and Colin assented, thinking it a very fine look indeed. Mark E Smith and his band had reaffirmed Colin's faith in rock 'n' roll bands by appearing in those peculiar hooded garments known as dufflecoats, which had not been hip since the nuclear disarmament dreamers knocked about in the streets. Colin, however, had been wearing a dufflecoat for ages, enduring consequent mockery and hardship galore. So he liked The Fall, and appreciated the noise it made. (In fact, though, Colin felt that the first time The Fall wasn't as good as it used to be was when its members stopped wearing dufflecoats.)

Alicia coughed. "So tell me about this Mark E Smith figure," she said, "or don't you know bugger all about him?" She smiled mischievously. "Ah, c'mon, you don't know bugger all, do you?"

"Well," Colin reddened slightly. He should've been used to her peculiar brand of teasing by now. He wasn't. "Mark E Smith was a docking clerk in Salford, which is in England somewhere, and he kinda latched onto the coattails of punk, sings a mix of rockabilly, Krautrock... Says he's influenced by Lou Reed, you know, one of the two main guys in the Velvets. The one who wasn't Welsh."

"Go on..."

"Well, he sings stuff about HP Lovecraft, Arthur

Machen… He was allegedly beset by ghosties and visions, he married a glamorous American blonde, he wrote a ballet about football, which is a less evolved form of rugby that English people like… He has this malady called 'Precog,' wherein he reckons he knows the future… You know, predictions you can only verify in retrospect, like last week's crosswords. Like that Nostradamus bloke. But it's largely spleen-venting songs he chooses to sing… Though he doesn't exactly sing, just kind of talks, really…"

She cocked an eyebrow. "You're feeding me a crock."

"No, no." Colin shooed Alicia back to her desktop terminal and guided her over to Alvin Snook's website.

She fell silent and began to read. Colin had intended for her to confirm his statements with merely a glance at the site. Instead, Sweet Alicia paid Colin no more mind whatsoever as, fascinated, she pored through WHO ARE THE FALL.[1] She proceeded to study bullet points underscored with Snook's pie charts, Venn diagrams, his maps of cheese, and the x-rays of song structures.

Unable to draw away her attention, Colin grew exceedingly impatient. He had always considered Snook to be ridiculous; now Colin was jealous. He finally cried out that he was off to America, that faraway land! Sweet Alicia did not look up.

Absorbed in the teachings of her computer, she dismissed Colin with a toss of her hand. (Not in the way you're thinking, though.)

The bell rang on his way out of the shop, too. This time it sounded harsh and derisive. Colin reminded himself not to take it too hard. He proceeded down the road a ways to the pub, where at this hour a few friends could reliably be found, some drinking through their lunch break, some drinking through their day. They loyally gathered for a brew called Brains Skull Attack (the closest they had to a hometown ale, as the brewery was located just twelve miles away in Cardiff).

"So," Colin told his mates as he knocked the skull against the hard oak bar of the pub. "Head of Pan told me to go to the City of New York this evening."

"At last," Sassy said gaily. She was consuming pickled eggs alongside brandy.

Sorry Ken was busy with the overhead TV, where men in shorts kicked a ball back and forth and back and forth, and then back and forth again. "I knew Pan would pipe up eventually," he grunted at Colin, and then returned to studying the football match.

Phil seemed the most gladdened by Colin's news. "Spring is here!" He was in his customary cowboy dress, a midnight-black coat over a white cotton shirt. He handed Colin the requisite pint of

Brains. "And a young man's thoughts turn to buggering Drew Barrymore." (Ms. Barrymore had married a local boy for all of three weeks; after their divorce, her name had wended its way into the curses of fair Gwent.)

Ken shifted from the TV and, upon Phil's behalf, apologized to all within earshot.

Phil threw back his shoulders. He raised his glass. "To New York!" he thundered. "Where superheroes blot out the sun!"

They clicked pints, with Pat joining in.

"New York," Colin added, "where King Kong died for our sins."

Ken belched. "Especially that sin of liking girls. Oh, sorry. That's not nice." He was embarrassed, per usual. "Argh, I'm sorry that I keep saying sorry. And sorry I said 'argh' just now. Argh. Sorry."

Sassy and Pat giggled and drained their Brains. *If only*, Colin thought again. Today the two girls appeared as children to him, more than usual, for they wore what looked like flower pajamas and teeny high-top sneakers, with their brunette hair tied up in topknots with green bows.

"They do lack a sense of irony," said Ken. He wiped his hands on his blue overalls. "The Americans. But they have better breakfasts than the British."

"You must look up Drew Barrymore," Phil winked, "though not in the way you're thinking."

Pat looked at him, her eyes wide as if in scandalous disbelief.

Ken apologized several more times.

"Honestly," Phil insisted. "Drew Barrymore. She lives there. And I have it on very good authority that she will let you have sex with her if you tell her what your mum and dad do for a living and then burst into tears."

"I'm sorry," Ken told Sassy and Pat for this.

"I appreciate the information." Colin took it quite earnestly. Then his face brightened. "Hey, did you know Sweet Alicia has the Necronicom?"

"Probably found it in a secondhand bookshop at Hay On Wye." Ken shrugged. "I'm sorry to say I got mine there."

Phil burst out laughing. "That isn't the *real* Necronicom. That's the one Jon Langford's brother Dave wrote."

"Jon Langford of the Mekonses?" asked Pat excitedly.

"Them Mekons, yeah."

"Sorry?" Ken's gaze hardened. He sounded defensive. "Dave's was quite close to the original."

Phil tipped his broad-brimmed hat to display his merry eyes. "What are you saying? It didn't have none of that supernatural thrust. It lacked the power to cloud men's minds, didn't open up the temporal gate. Nothing like that."

Colin helped himself to a nibble from one of Sassy's treacle tarts and addressed Pat. "So. Turns out when Pan speaks, the skull becomes very warm. Unbearably so. You can't even hold it. Finally threw it in the freezer, that's what I had to do."

There was a long pause.

"Still," Ken muttered, "I'm sorry, but Dave's Necronicom *is* readily available in paperback." He edged away to become engrossed again in the football match. The men in shorts had finished their little break. They now regrouped on the TV screen to kick the ball back and forth for the second half of the so-called game.

"Yeah, well," declared Colin. "Alicia has the real thing. It's under her bed."

"That's funny," said Pat, "I always figured Eartha Kitt had the Necronicom and read through it to get in character for Catwoman."

Sassy nodded. "I heard that Keith Chegwin's descent into alcoholism was a result of the Necronicom which found its way onto *Multi-Coloured Swapshop*."

Colin vehemently shook his head. "Them were each bootleg Necronicoms. Sweet Alicia's is the Wormius edition that Hess brought over. Her dad nicked it off Churchill."

"And no one noticed?" Phil sneered. He was always the great skeptician. (In the movie, he would have to be played by Scully off *The X-Files*, the only one, gender notwithstanding, who could muster up the requisite air of skepticiousness when confronted by mind-altering coincidences.)

"Sure," said Colin, "it caused that minor occult war documented in the suppressed issue of *Swamp Thing* that your Dad gave you. Last summer. Remember?"

Phil was abashed. "Oh, that."

They fell quiet for a bunch of time, appreciating the comforts of the boisterous pub: the tinkling of ice in long glasses and the dull murmurs of wussy students feeling sorry for themselves. Most were young English unfortunates adrift in these savage northwestern parts. The students were less there than ghosts. (This is natural, for the saying goes that those whom the gods wish to destroy are sent to be raised in England.)

(Wales, on the other hand, is today's Athens. Athletic in build, Byronic in spirit, its citizens stroll the nation's balmy boulevards and discuss the great issues of the day, pausing only to admire some new architectural marvel. The civic buildings of this land exude a knowing grandeur, an ongoing testament to the wisdom and foresight of the elders. A tolerant, open-hearted, generous people who have dedicated their lives to the pursuit and exaltation of beauty, the Welsh are noted for high spirits and excited behavior. They share with their Celtic forefathers a fondness for feasting, drinking, and quarreling.)

"Oh, Colin!" Pat suddenly remembered some

very happy news. "Our friend Teleri has fallen in love with you! She says she saw you down at the Civic Centre yesterday and next thing she saw a porpoise in the harbor."

"That's nice," responded Colin. As the most eligible bachelor amid the most romantic peoples, Colin got this a lot. *Them Tom Cruise eyes*, women were apt to swoon as he happened past. *Feast your gaze, ladies, on the Antonio Banderas of Wales, our very own Mellie Gibson! Aaah — !* Some would dive for a souvenir patch off his Jean Claude Van Damme-like bottom or grab at a loose button that could be kept. Just now, Colin remembered their friend Teleri as a cheap harlot in denim trousers. "I'm pleased to hear that."

"Yes, I can tell," Sassy drily observed, though she then patted his cheek without reproach. She gave a crooked smile and said, forgivingly, "You foolishly handsome boy."

"So," Pat changed the subject, "you're seeing The Fall?"

"Yeah, I am." Colin scooted over slightly and joined Ken in gazing up at the match.

"You know," Ken said, "it's not as good as it used to be."

"What, football? What used to happen then? Some excitement, was there?"

"I meant The Fall."

"Not as good as it used to be? But 'twas just last Christmas at Bristol that you leapt onto the stage to smooch Mark E Smith."

Ken winced and turned away. Argh, the friends who feel they always must remind you of the things drink makes you do.

"Once it enlisted Mark Smith's wife," interjected Phil, "The Fall was not as good as it used to be."

"Ha," went Colin. "Once the band got some right proper rock star clothes it was not as good as it used to be."

"Still," asked Sassy, with a fervent sort of loyalty, "who else has gone twenty years doing nuts perverse stuff what no one understands?"

The boys ignored her. "I'll tell you another thing," Phil said. "There is a record called *Bread On The Night* by Liverpool Scene. Made in 1968. On this record is a track called 'The Entry Of Christ Into Liverpool.' That track, so help me, is The Fall nine years early."

Colin and his mates often thought about The Fall so much they got headaches and had to masturbate just so's they could think of something else.

The game on the television ended. Sorry Ken lit up a smelly imported cigarette in victory. "The worst disappointment," he insisted, "was when it brought out *The Light User Syndrome* two years ago. This made me realize that something was not quite right in The Fall. Up until *The Light User Syndrome*, I would say The Fall had never let me down, had never made a bad album. It had made greater and lesser albums, but they were all worth buying. But this sounded — "

"Like indie wuss music," said Colin, "yeah. It even had a crap title, like something British Bastard Telecom would put in one of their shitty brochures."

"Nowadays it is just not as good as it used to be."

Pat had a smelly imported cigarette, too. "Who among us is?"

"I was a lapsed fan," Sassy testified, "until I saw The Fall last Xmas. Really good, but Smiffy was well messing about with everybody's guitars and stuff."

"Say, now. Wasn't that the time Ken jumped onstage to smooch Mark E Smith?" laughed Pat. They were always having a go at him for smooching Smiffy.

"Bastards," said Ken. "No, you're right. I'm sorry," he said for the 1,057,312th time in his life, and the 43rd time that afternoon.

A nearby pub patron rustled through a copy of the *Western Mail*.

A few cribbage players shuffled decks of cards.

Some of the students who had been watching the football match held fervent discussions, as English football fans do. "We would have won if we had scored another goal and you had scored one less," somebody reasoned in a shrill voice. They were always saying stuff like that, were football fans. "Well, if he hadn't missed he would have scored then we would have won and you would have lost." With monotonous regularity, someone mentioned that England won the World Cup in 1966, and they all stood for a quick round of "God Save the Queen."

Colin—who believed football a pursuit second only to opera in sheer daftness—often wished he could somehow jump the space-time continuum and deflect Sir Geoff's hat trick on that overblown July 30 back at Wembley. He consoled himself with the certainty that England had lost the 1966 World Cup in some parallel continuum, and attempted to render a sketch of Sassy's green bow upon his cocktail napkin. "When I see *The Light User Syndrome* in record shops," Colin said, "priced £14.60 or so, I get a faint urge to purchase it, and thereby have everything by The Fall. But to do so would make me a completist."

"A truly sad bastard."

"A pathetic fate, a record collector; like a trainspotter, or someone who supports a football team."

"Fuck off," said Ken. "Argh. Sorry."

"Just buy it," Phil said, "when it makes you a reasonable offer. When it turns up at a rate commensurate with what you consider its value."

"Which is, oh," Colin did some quick mental math, "two pounds."

"I tell you," said Phil, crumbling up Colin's

illustration dejectedly and setting the napkin aflame in the ashtray. "When The Fall started dilly-dallying with all of those ballet people, with Leigh Bowery and Michael Clarke, that was actually when it first disappointed me. Those people were just talentless bums, whom The Fall should have had no truck with whatsoever. Anyone can put on a fucking leotard and paint spots on his face." Phil picked up a near-empty beer glass and, as fans of The Fall are apt to do, repeated his last sentence into the beer glass using a Mark E Smith voice. "Anyone-*aa* can put on a fucking leotard-*uh* and paint spots... on his... *face*."

This was yet another example of a way in which The Fall was not like other groups. When Fall fans uttered any suitably Smith-esque sentence, they invariably reached for beer glasses into which they'd imitate the lead singer. This was such commonplace behavior that none regarded it as the least bit noteworthy.

"Objectively," Pat said, "a lot of what The Fall has done is, objectively, absolute piffle." Already Pat was drunk. "I mean why do we like it? We can't really say, can we?" She playfully undid Ken's string tie, which he immediately retied.

"I just want to return to the question of how The Fall is not like other groups," interrupted Colin. "I notice it keeps coming up." He paused to blow on the ashes of his drawing. "Kazoos is the one way that The Fall is not like others. No one else ever used kazoos, except the Mothers of Invention. First band I ever saw, the Mothers. Mooched off school, appropriately enough, to see a matinee. People thought I was making it up because what I said I'd seen sounded too cool. I was disappointed in bands for years to come. 'But they don't play no RUBBERCHICKENS!! They don't make no SNORKS!!'"

"Say," Sorry Ken pointed out the pub's timepiece, "hadn't you be off soon, if you're due in America tonight?"

"Right, right. Well, everyone. I'll see you in my dr—"

"Dearie!" Sassy shook him by the shoulder. "Don't forget to play the diddler before you go!"

She shoved him in the direction of the slot machines.

"Jesus, where is my memory?" Colin was dismayed. "Thanks for reminding me."

With beer in hand, Colin tramped to the corner where the one-armed bandits awaited. His mates tagged along, eager to watch someone at long last beat these goddamn thieving English machines.

"Okay, here goes." He picked a slot at random. "Wish me luck."

"You need luck?" scoffed Ken.

"Yeah," Phil said, "your skull's got it all fixed, don't it?"

"Wish me luck." Colin sighed. "It's just an expression."

Pat brought her face close to his. "Buy us a pint with your winnings?"

"Wish I could, love."

"I wish someone would buy her Brains," Sorry Ken joked. He apologized, but not before earning a sharp elbow in the ribs.

"C'mon, Pat!" said Phil. "Colin's going to the Land of the Free. He'll need his money there."

"I suppose," Pat relented, "and it could be worse. He could be going to England."

Colin inserted a coin and yanked on the machine's arm. The painted fruit blurred, round and round, then fell suddenly into place. A siren went off. Lights flashed. A slew of coins avalanched out the bottom dispenser.

"Oh, what a surprise," murmured Ken.

"Lookie, " Colin couldn't hide his glee. "I scored me the jackpot."

"Well, well!" Phil hollered. "Look at that everyone!"

Patrons all about the pub cheered and saluted Colin with raised pints. Several began to sing "For He's A Jolly Good Fellow" but, failing to settle on the key or any sort of tempo, they shut up after a few shattered lines and returned to their pints.

"Alright," said Sorry Ken, "so that's enough for a one-way ticket. But how you getting back?"

"Uh." Colin had actually given it scant thought. "Pan will provide, I suppose, just as sure as he provides his special cakes every pancake day."

"Maybe more slots. They got gambling there," Sassy pointed out, "after all."

"Oh, do they ever!" laughed Pat.

"Just don't get stuck in that America," warned Ken. "Look what it's done to our Jonny Langford."

"What?" Phil asked. "Made him a famous painter?"

"Okay," said Colin, "now I'm really off—"

"No luggage?" Apparently Sorry Ken possessed all the sticky questions today.

"Oh, well. Guess not. I mean, Pan... He would've told me to bring luggage. Right?"

"Don't ask me. I'm no expert on communicating with them deceased deities."

Colin snickered. His friends walked him out to the street. They stood by until the cab arrived to take him to the Newport Airport.

Sassy pecked him on the cheek. "Goodbye, Ambassador!"

"Have a jolly time," said Phil. He shook Colin's hand, as did Ken.

Pat smiled sadly. "Return soon."

"You'll still be here when I come back, right?" Colin gave her a hug. "You won't have run off to the land of the Scots again?"

"Oh, sure. I'll be here. Right in there. On my three hundred and fiftieth pint of Brains. Might be passed out on the floor, but I'll be here."

They waved.

He was off.

In new york, Clarke had at last broken free of Brandon's loopy, circuitous shouting. He sat in his office, worn-out and chilled, unable to do much but tremble. All day he read up on The Fall as he awaited the return of Fredericks and Hopper.

"The subject (mes) changes line-ups monthly," read the dossier open before him.

He fires managers and record companies. His songs are lists of put-downs. His is the complainer's life. There are no other rock stars like MES—the few with his bile lack his longevity. Similar to Fidel Castro, he outlives expectation while delighting in his island of hostility. MES persistently refuses to accept easy outs. Since forcing his way into the public eye at age nineteen, his confidence and drive seem never to've waned. In his songs, there are riots, ghosts, murders. In his interviews, he stews. Politics are bankrupt; religion, philosophy, and poetry are bankrupt. Only pop music will have MES.

The followers of MES are characterized by the symptoms and signs of a cult of personality. The most common presenting symptom of any Fall fan is a disappointment in "ordinary folks" and in what is surrendered daily in exchange for pleasure and convenience. No language is incendiary enough for MES followers. Praise or insults that shy away from absolute terms are deemed cowardly and false. Their small hearts fill with secret glee when learning a new insult. To be right is all that matters to them. Convulsive seizures rarely occur. Their pantheon is packed with sour eggheads, cutthroat intellectuals, arithmetic bullies. Go soft on an answer, go vague on a detail, go easy on an underachiever, and, to the eyes of an MES follower, you are dead. Their hero can dismiss anyone, at any time, for the slightest offense, on a whim. A favorite painter might weaken at the easel momentarily, an approved politician succumb to monetary temptations, a leading authority state something wrong, an admired author pen some mere entertainment. There is no forgiveness, as corticobulbar pathways of emotional control seem to be affected by adoration of MES.

Euphoria occurs in some fans; a reactive depression, in others. Theirs is a Robespierre mindset. Strangers can be dismissed on the flimsiest pretexts—they can have the right idea expressed in the right way but if it arrives in the wrong shoes, well gosh, sorry. Not just people, but whole households can be written off, neighborhoods, provinces, hemispheres. Mild emotional disturbances among MES followers often suggest the incorrect initial impression of hysteria. Subtle distinctions weigh heavily on them, brutal notions like "principles" and "integrity." They are commonly at an age when the loneliness of such a lifestyle remains unfathomable. Followers of MES can be imagined disputing late in the cafe nights, lunging at one another over an idle comment that hints, in that instant, at utter betrayal, knocking over chairs, tables, and beer pitchers in passion and haste. In a flash, their academic discourses can flare into brawls, into street battles, and, potentially, even guerrilla warfare.

Also, they are wont to "do the voice" into half-empty beer glasses at a moment's notice…

Presently, Clarke grew detached from his assigned reading and fell into a troubled abstraction. His mind strayed back to the visitors, to their warnings about Vaughn. *So this is how it happens*, he thought. Like in high school, when the wrestling coach disallowed the team from having girlfriends, termed them distractions, drains. Clarke laid his head down on his desk. What makes a friendship? How many true friends did he have left? He had sworn fealty to many people and completely meant it, but then over time had gotten distracted, sobered up, drifted off, people he had loved but couldn't stomach, or despicable people he had envied to whom he had tried to get close. If, as Geoffrey Sonnabend has written, the true by-product of life is forgetting, not remembering, then it followed that the loss of friendships was the most natural consequence of life, more so than the accrual and maintenance of friendships. Unless…

Where were these men from? Why didn't he look closer at their badges? Why the strange clothes? Were they yet another regulatory agency violating the constitution's checks and balances, privately charged with the task of sorting Americans into colleagues, chums, companions, acquaintances, lovers? Could it be? And where had his own best friends gone off to, Carl Coughlin from high school, freckly and muscular, they had been as close as could be, they lit one another's Lucky Strikes, they changed clothes in one another's presence, but then after Carl moved back to NYC… how had they lost touch? What about Greg from the neighborhood, that droll boy with his devastating wordplays, his fantastic generosity?

From his desk, Clarke rotated to look searchingly out the window, where the light was broken-up and dimming. The dusk bore many small clouds.

The Seagram Building gleamed.

If rumors were true, deals emanating from Seagram's bronze and glass high-rise might soon form the world's largest entertainment conglomerate. Until recently a liquor company, Seagram's would imminently own twenty-five percent of the us music business. This included Brandon's label. Clarke was plenty familiar with the subsequent routine: a takeover, the cutbacks, the winnowing of rosters. Mergers are good for business, bad for music. Brandon was over in that glass box right now, seated behind the Picasso in The Four Seasons, pleading with some tycoon's accountant for his job. Clarke's fate, along with the fate of American culture, was being determined over cocktails in the Pool Room.

Clarke returned to his reading, tried once more to concentrate on the thick packet of Fall information, his homework for tonight's gig. He flipped listlessly through the manila folder, glanced at one Fall review[2], then another[3], then a story or something.[4]

A thought occurred to him. Could it be these men had also visited people from his own life?

This would explain a lot, someone meeting his pals behind his back to convince them that he, Clarke, was an asshole, playing them surveillance tapes which revealed his true nature, one of duplicity and cruelty, of fantastic disregard for others. They'd dog his footsteps, lace up detonators, sink his friendships without a trace.

In fact, were they only pretending that this was about Vaughn, that nobody? Much more likely it was directed at Clarke, a man on the inside of a tremendously profitable enterprise. Those e-mails that warned everyone in the company how easily secrets could be stolen by industrial saboteurs... well, why bother with secrets, this would be sabotage enough, it would fix everything—take away an employee's friends and then ask him to put in a useful day at work, it couldn't be done, no way.

His paranoia drifted on, accompanied by the rumble of distant trucks and trains. After a time, a buzzer sounded. He jerked from his reverie. "Clarke!" squawked Brandon through the intercom. "I'm in the street. Come on, fuckhead. We're late for the fucking Brownie's show. I'm double parked." Realizing the time, Clarke was disconcerted. Alice, his secretary, had departed hours ago. He slowly donned his jacket, shook off his sleepiness. Before heading downstairs, Clarke gave another glance at the evening outside.

He shivered.

The horizon looked bloody where jets sliced the air.

FLYING JUST THEN over the apparently eternal Atlantic, Colin B Morton settled back on a miniature pillow and rested his eyes. He felt tired. His certainties had stampeded away like so many Who fans. With total faith in what once was holy, taking the word of the skull of a god, Colin had boarded a flight from Newport to New York via Manchester. He'd been overwhelmed — then admittedly titillated — but now exhausted — to find that travelling to America was plainly so different than what he'd anticipated. The naked in-flight shuffleboard and the strip keno had caught him utterly by surprise. And then the S&M spelling bee... With the trip now almost over, Colin was emptied of expectation. The whole airplane stank of condoms and cologne. On this early April dusk, in the encroaching gloom, he felt completely cut off, swaddled in the engine roar, on a distant craft. Yet another nubile stewardess tapped his shoulder. Evidently, it was Colin's turn to do a pornographic karaoke number. Eyes shut tightly, he pulled away and emitted a snore. The stewardess moved on. A hedonistic passenger across the aisle performed in Colin's stead. "Up in Hafodrynys where the Taffies dig for coal," sang the hedonist with gusto, "a Taffy shoved a shovel up another Taffy's hole…" Still, Colin rested, refusing to look. Perhaps he was dreaming.

Some time later, as they descended for the landing, Colin awoke. New York was growing outside the plane window. Though seeing it for the first time, Colin already recognized the place from comic books. In the distance, he imagined the Golden Golfer arcing golf balls toward the sinister sky.[5]

"Thank you for joining us today," the captain declared, as the plane bounced on the tarmac. "This pleasure flight has been brought to you by Pan American. Let's all give it up for the Great God!"

Departing the airplane, Colin frantically sought a cold fountain in which to bathe Pan's head, for it had begun to glow, in the pocket of his dufflecoat, with a heated sort of gratification. Colin felt it burning against his upper thigh. Colin was only now realizing how much Pan liked to party.

He was intercepted in his mad dash by a bloke in an immigration hat. "Excuse me," declared Bloke in Hat, "we have questions regarding your country of origin."

"Yes?"

"On the form, you put down 'Wales' as your country of origin. Am I correct?"

"Yep."

"I'm sorry. In this case, you'll have to put down 'UK.'"

"*You're sorry?* Listen. Maybe you have got yourself a very sharp nifty hat and costume, mate, but that won't make the United Kingdom a country."

"Ah. Well. England. Wales." Hat-bloke looked up. "Really, what's the difference?"

"The same as the difference between American and Native American," sneered Colin.

"I don't get you."

"Look. It's… it's a Welsh thing."

Colin felt the temperature of Pan rise a few more degrees. A moment of dark magic took place, a convenient hypnosis. The hatted bloke looked suddenly drunk, robbed of any will. He staggered off into the terminal.

A similar thing occurred when Colin hailed a taxicab. "Where you headed?" grunted the driver, as they pulled away from JFK. Colin made no reply. Instead, he extracted the skull and placed it alongside him on the back seat. Immediately, some sort of spell was cast. The cabbie tore through traffic entranced. Without speaking, he drove them straight into the city. Meanwhile, the head of Pan smoldered such that it melted the back seat's upholstery. The yellow cab filled with the smoky, biting smell of burnt polyurethane. The driver braked before a nightclub in the East Village. Colin checked to see how much he owed but the taxi's meter had been halted at zero. He pried up Pan's head, a difficult task as the underside of the skull was now lined with a gooey wad of vinyl; it was a bit like yanking something out of a very cheesy, blue pizza. "Thank you," said Colin as he exited. The cabbie wordlessly pulled away.

Colin re-pocketed the skull and headed into Brownie's.

There was a woman standing like a stick insect outside on the sidewalk. There is always a woman like a stick insect standing outside such places. No one knows why.

THE MIDTOWN CONVENTION of bank managers had wound down too early. By 6:35 in the evening, Betsy Randell found herself back in her hotel room on Forty-Ninth Street. She had dined, purchased souvenirs, and mailed postcards. She had packed and repacked her suitcase several times. She had nothing left to do. Her departure from Newark lay sixteen hours in the future — or, to be precise, fifteen hours and thirty-nine minutes. She employed eight and a half minutes cogitating upon her dilemma. She then took the elevator down five floors, bought a weekly paper in the lobby for seventy-five cents, and returned to her room by 7:06. Twenty-two minutes were thence occupied perusing movie advertisements without any conclusion. At approximately 7:31, she unfolded the middle section of the paper to discover a list of recommended picks. She scanned the list with only moderate interest until, after two minutes, she came across the following:

THE FALL

Ranting raconteur and iconoclastic curmudg-icon Mark E Smith ("the thin[king] man's David Thomas" - Cocksucker Blues Fanzine) brings The Fall to another East Village venue. After last week's raucous gig at Coney Island High, only one thing can be assured: expect the unexpected.

10:30 PM
Brownie's, 169 Avenue A
$8.00

The notion of catching The Fall in concert struck her just then with a quaint nostalgia. It would be like seeing The B-52s with all its dead members, in their original hair, or listening to any of the records she heard when visiting at John and Kevin's nearly twenty years ago.

There next occurred a moment such as she scarcely experienced any longer during which Betsy Randell, losing all track of time, indulged herself in sentimental reminiscence. During that moment, she recalled seeing The Fall before, in LA, in the late Seventies, or maybe the early Eighties. Maybe another time as well. Maybe just that once. She drank a lot in those days, mostly gin with Mountain Dew. Betsy remembered it was

47

at a twenty-one-or-over club. Helen pressed her
for a ride to the show but had a bitch of a time
getting in. Helen wasn't even in high school yet.
As the elder of their circle, Betsy purchased the
intoxicants. They took her vw, sat in a downtown
lot surrounded by high dark buildings, inhaled
N_2O from balloons. A new Fall record had just
come out the day before, it was a small ten inch.
The cover was yellow. Helen had listened to it at
John and Kevin's, smoking cigarettes and nodding
along. The boys had opted for The Germs at the
Stardust Ballroom instead of this show. They
might show up later, assuming they could get in.
They were only seventeen. Helen was stubborn,
determined to see The Fall perform. This is what
made her so sexy, even then, just entering her
teens: her determination. The Fall pulled up in a
white American van, parked near the stage
entrance, slowly tumbled out. There were other
kids, also too young to enter the club. These
others went up to Kay, the band's manager, who
seemed nice but unremarkable, like a mom or a
substitute teacher. They asked Kay to keep The
Fall outside while they employed a street action to
force open the doors for those who were
underage. Kay couldn't understand their plan but
it sounded very detailed. At the honk of a car
horn, these six rush this door, those three block
that fire exit, the rest go here and start doing this
and then something else. They assured her it'd

already succeeded at many shows in the Southland. They implied that the band should not play until the concert had been transformed into an all ages show. There were a fair number of youngsters, little Californian boys overdressed in leather and trench coats and mod parkas, stuck there outside in the parking lot, maybe eighteen or twenty, but not so many that their attendance would help make the show significantly more profitable. Kay said she couldn't see The Fall going along with that scheme, nope. Helen too was opposed because of her distrust of anything that bore a collective stamp, stupid clarion calls for cooperation. Her huge junior high had already taught her to despise group dynamics because they led, as with TV's contents, to averaging, rule by lowest common denominator. At thirteen she didn't know everything but she knew that The Fall was not about being average. Helen broke from the pack in the parking lot and directly approached the band's singer, Mark. Mark was, to put it politely, thinking about something else. He was staring at the building from a distance of several inches and poking at a dent in the cinderblock with a slender, shaky finger. He was not rude so much as drugged, probably amphetamines. Not a surprise, when Helen recalled hearing the "Rowche Rumble" 45 at John and Kevin's: "*Beer and speed are alright!*" Mark wore a long-sleeved shirt with a wide collar tucked loosely into a pair of plain jeans. He was thin, much too thin, exhausted and fidgety. He stank. He had his hair parted on the left, shoulder-length in back. It seemed he had styled it after dunking his head into a pail of motor oil. She could still see the lines left by the comb as with greaseheads in the Fifties. His ears and chin stuck out. "Hi. I'm too young. Could I carry some instrument inside for you and pretend to be your roadie so I can sneak in?" Mark wouldn't look at her. He tried to answer, swallowed. The way he tightly clenched his jaw, like Kevin did when he did black beauties, so that his cheeks were sucked in and his lips pursed, reminded her of a cud-chewing cow. "We already," she heard Mark softly mutter, "took it all in." He frowned, but couldn't seem to tear his stare away from the wall of the building. Eventually Betsy and Helen solved it without anybody else's help. Betsy went into the show, flung her ID out the third-floor bathroom window and into the parking lot. How erratically it tumbled down, as if determined to escape Helen's grasp. Then Helen entered, claiming to be Betsy Randell, making two in attendance that night. It was a fantastic show. The Fall played mostly older songs. Mark chanted lots of new words and got very sweaty. He kept his back to the audience. Phranc, famous lesbian folksinger, was in the audience along with most every luminary in the LA scene (X, Los Lobos, The Blasters). Helen

50

got Phranc's autograph on a bar napkin for Betsy ("More power to our elbows! Luv, Phranc"). A famous lesbian! Then on the way home from the show, Betsy's vw died. It was two in the morning. They got it to the side of the road and put on their hazards. A middle-aged man stopped. He was nice but unremarkable, like a clerk or a shop teacher. He tested the gas pedal, crawled beneath the car, diagnosed a break in the wire between the accelerator and the engine. He manipulated the carburetor while they turned over the ignition, then he tied open the throttle with a shoelace and told them not to shift from second until they got home.

It was 8:02 in New York now as Betsy pondered, for the first time in too long, where Helen had gone. She'd heard Kevin managed a restaurant. John had become a glass blower in Nevada. No one talked about Helen, or even the folksinger Phranc, these days. People are always telling about the men. Makes it that much easier to lose the women. Tonight, for example, Betsy could see The Fall… but would she ever be able to attend a Phranc concert anymore?

Again, Betsy Randell unpacked her suitcase. She selected from her wardrobe a pair of gray slacks and black loafers. She donned a gray sweater dotted with pale roses. She regarded herself in the mirror and thought, *I got a waist like a turnip*. The time was 8:16. She took everything off. She telephoned downstairs to ascertain how long it would take to ride the subway to First Avenue and then she put all her clothes back on again. She contemplated packing up her suitcase, decided against it. She did it anyway. She checked her watch against the room clock. Frustrating. One was slow or one was fast. At 9:08, she once more unpacked her suitcase. Again she dressed in the gray slacks and sweater, the black loafers. She tried on a red scarf. She became convinced that it adequately distracted from her vague and lumpy shape. At 9:23, full of swagger and conviction, she headed out.

The clock in the lobby said 9:55. She conferred with the desk clerk to confirm that the hotel's clock was indeed running about thirty-two minutes fast. She also re-confirmed with several people the length of time that it would take to get to First Avenue.

The clock in the street said 6:14. She asked several passers-by for the time, but none were wearing watches. On the subway platform there were two overhead clocks; one said 3:29, the other said 10:10. She was becoming flustered. She'd forgotten to take her medicine. She thought about returning for it. She considered retiring to her hotel room for the rest of the night. She considered changing clothes. She looked around the subway car at the many fashionable individuals. She fretted about being inappropriately attired. She asked someone for the time. They scowled and ignored her.

She realized then that she had left her suitcase wide open. As if she didn't already have enough weighing on her! She jumped out at the next stop and caught the subway heading back uptown. She passed all the broken clocks, trying not to hear what they were saying. She ran back up to her hotel room. She packed up her suitcase and locked it. She then placed the suitcase in her closet and locked that. She re-traced her steps to the subway, got on a train, and again felt embarrassed for what she was wearing. She asked a policeman for the time and he reassured her that yes, it truly was 10:45, as her watch said. She flushed with delight and smiled appreciatively at him. She transferred to the L, going east along Fourteenth. As she neared her destination, she imagined how easily a thief could break into her hotel room—into her closet—into her suitcase. It wouldn't take much skill! The overhead clock at First Avenue said 2:38. She climbed the steps toward the street. She realized that, in returning to her hotel room, she had still forgotten to take her medicine. She froze in fright. Just then her eye was caught by the electronic readout on a nearby bank façade. It said the time was 11:12. Her watch was right! Betsy Randell felt like skipping; instead, she sauntered.

She came upon Brownie's, still feeling great.

WITH CLARKE BEHIND THE WHEEL of the company car, Brandon brooded in the back seat. For the first time, the head of the label was completely quiet.

Clarke steered south on Park Avenue. "So," he asked casually. He could no longer contain his interest. "How'd the meeting at The Four Seasons go?"

"I felt like the fucking Emperor of Japan surrendering to that shithead MacArthur."

"You still have a label?"

"Yeah," Brandon groaned. None of this was easy. Every step of the way he met resistance. He had started this label to shepherd music into the future. Guitars and all their incessant chord changes went with the past, when people went about naked and banged on books or whatever they did before electricity. Dead sounds! The future was jump-cuts, the future was soon to be available on video, the future was electronic, the future was in bits, the future was surging, charging, it was high-voltage dance floors, lengthy antennas, squawky-talkies, platform tie pianos, the future was sparking to life in the corner of a

Radio Shack while the past still employed dreary parlor charades to make lame crotch-thrusting, hair-tossing, word-spouting guitar bands seem relevant. Electronic artists were pioneers! Down with people in music! "Yeah, I still have a fucking label. I still have a fucking job. But you don't, it looks like."

"Me?"

"Right."

"What did I do?"

"Shit. Remember the CD with the promotional frog… What was that CD called?"

"*Frog*."

"Yeah."

"Of course, I remember."

"So do the cocksuckers. So do the bean counters at Seagram's."

"But Frog was yours. You won the bid. You signed Frog."

"Possibly. But the promotion was entirely your fucking idea! That's how the cocksuckers see it. But you still got at least six months with me. There's a sort of forum for appeals in these situations. There's wiggle room. I'll keep negotiating."

"Okay."

"Also, the fucks had something against an essay you wrote in college. About a conspiracy to sabotage some loser named… uh, Colonel Sanders… no, not him. Who was it? Oh, yeah.

Captain Beefheart."

"They saw that?"

"Seagram's sees all."

Clarke cursed softly as he studied the world through the windshield. This entire landscape, once housing countless companies, now belonged to a handful of businesses (QVC, AOL, MCA, ABC) and sickos (Turner, Eisner, Redstone, Murdoch). Manhattan was merely a series of wholly owned subsidiaries. Essentially, the city's architecture was being gutted, after which only the Seagram Building, and perhaps the Bertelsmann skyscraper, would remain intact.

"But I didn't necessarily call it 'sabotage.' I just expressed a pet theory that *Trout Mask Replica* has actually sold millions."

In the back of the car, Brandon jerked upright. He looked around wildly and roared, even louder than usual, "THE FUCK YOU DID!"

"But listen a second. What if the record companies are suppressing this—"

"YOU'RE RIDICULOUS, ASSHOLE!"

"Because they don't want *Trout Mask Replica* to become an industry benchmark—"

"YOU'RE TALKING BULLSHIT!—Asshole, you hear me?! A conspiracy? IMPOSSIBLE! Nothing like that—you listening?! IT COULDN'T HAPPEN. And even if it did... BUT IT COULDN'T!"

"Because then the record companies will have to figure out a way to replicate the strange brilliance of *Trout Mask Replica*. Which isn't possible."

"Must I remind you, Clarke, that THERE IS NO 'THEY' ANYMORE. *We* are the record companies. Got it? Have I EVER ONCE shown you ANY EVIDENCE of such collusion? OF COURSE NOT. So just SHUT THE FUCK UP and turn the radio on real GODDAMN LOUD and STOP TALKING and let's appreciate some fucking childish noise."

Clarke did as he was instructed. At Twelfth near Second, he turned into a parking garage. Brandon continued to fume. They walked, absorbed in awkward silence. They came within sight of Alphabet City. All at once, Clarke shuddered with affection for Vaughn. This was his neighborhood. Whatever trouble he was in, whatever he was about to become... Clarke just hoped his friend was doing okay.

VAUGHN LIKED TO STAND like a scarecrow amidst the dusty dog run of Tompkins Square Park, searching for something he couldn't place, abuzz and motionless while a billion domesticated animals buffeted past, snarling, wagging, barking, bowing, nuzzling, sniffing, momentarily liberated, their licenses ringing loudly against the nametags on their choke collars.

Puerto Ricans possessed purebreds, mostly

short hair things with strength and speed, they leashed their dogs' necks tightly with motorcycle belts, called them Chuy, Fe, Tito. Ukrainians named their large, friendly yellow dogs Alya or Georgy. The Irish owned pointy-snouted pups or Japanese breeds, one or two had those drooling dogs with big jowls, Brazilians had fighting dogs, a few known as rescue dogs, one that looked like a cartoon, all of them titled after Biblical personages. The college kids made pets out of pound runts with names like Pogo, Offisa Pup, with ears limp and furry as gourmet mushrooms, their wet, black noses like olives. They stole one another's jingle balls and ran tight laps around the enclosure. A billion dog parents enforced a billion codes of screwy behavior, revealing everything about themselves in the way they met the dogs without greeting the parents, the way they cared or didn't care about a pile of vomit or some crap or how roughly their dog chewed another's ear.

Vaughn liked to catch the F train at First Avenue on Saturdays and Sundays like he was boarding a ground rocket intent on a new land speed record, shooting to Brooklyn blind in a tunnel beneath blast-off-like G forces, intuiting the heaviness of waterways overhead as they traveled under the East River at velocities heretofore unimaginable and then surfacing to see the dead trophy they'd dropped in the harbor, that

Statue of Liberty, the green creature in the lagoon, distant and drowning. Thousands got on, thousands got off. He had a moment to draw a breath at Coney Island before the ride started over again.

He would travel sometimes all weekend that way, searching for something he couldn't place, watching dignified, gold-toothed Mexicans from El Barrio sell day-old flower bouquets and one-dollar items from shopping carts, the black-haired Korean dry cleaners who'd get on with their manicurist wives and slurp bone soups out of plastic containers, Jackson Height Colombians in shorts and cleats hugging soccer balls to their chests. Boys from Barbados in dreadlocks could be heard peddling Polaroids of the Lion of Judah. He'd watch Lebanese wives from Bay Ridge sweating terribly in head scarves and long shapeless dresses. All this, in the dank subway screech, while above ground in this cosmopolitan capital of chaos coffee-skinned men strode the streets of Bois Verna singing love songs in Creole, physical therapists dined on suckling pig, garment workers lit candles in Buddhist altars, spirit seekers bought amulets from botanicas, and Greeks hurled their dinner plates to the restaurant floor as if in disgust.

Vaughn liked to go for Indian food on Sixth Street in a very narrow restaurant candied with layer upon layer of glitter beads and flashing

lights and colored bulbs. It was something
instantly religious, like being penned up inside
the holding cell of a blinking, pulsing spacecraft.
The front of his brain received something on the
order of fifty thousand watts from the experience.
He went so often, eating sumptuous rogan josh to
the tuneless plucking of ancient instruments, that
his archeological cohorts at the Institute
complained he smelled of the spices, of cumins,
curries, and coriander, it was on his breath, in his
hair, his clothes, he was dragging it all around the
workplace and keeping them from doing their
jobs, and they said he could go for dinner, but
insisted he had to stop eating Indian for lunch.

One night, Vaughn, in his restaurant, overheard
a couple.

"It's okay to believe in not killing," a woman's
voice was saying, "even in not killing Pol Pot."

"Is it," the man collected his thoughts before
continuing, "okay to believe in eating Pol Pot for
lunch?"

"Yes, but only if he's already dead."

"Uh-oh."

"Too late, huh?"

There was a guilty pause. "Kinda."

"Bon appetit."

"I think, could it be, I may've caught a little
buzz from ingesting Pol Pot. Or does that only
happen if he's smoked?"

Vaughn turned in his chair to observe who was

speaking. A difficult task. One could discern only pieces of the faces of the other customers, a raised eyebrow, the left half of a grimace, through the shiny tendrils of foil, the loose ends of ornaments dangling from the ceiling's low wooden cross-beams, the inconstant Casino-soul lighting. That's what was so special about this place, the impenetrable jungle of decorations.

"So," the woman was asking, "what did you think of my bulimia article?"

"Oh, Lady Millhauser… You won't believe this. I've been so hungry I couldn't read your bulimia article."

"Camden!"

"I know, I know. I'm sorry. Too hungry to read about bulimia. Somewhere a dog is laughing at this cosmic justice. No, a god, that's what I mean. Jesus! A dog, I would eat."

"Eat some of this nan, for dog's sake."

"Ach! I can stand nan of it."

"Authors eating dogs! Is nothing safe in this world?"

"I'd eat an author, if they'd just eaten a dog, who'd just eaten an order of nan."

"Would you eat an order of nan that had just eaten an author? A big order, a small author."

"Is there dog involved somewhere? Like in the seasoning or preparing?"

So Camden was an author, and Lady Millhauser, apparently, a journalist. Vaughn took a sip of water, caught a sudden reflection of the couple in his silverware. They were squeezed into the table directly back of his, so near to Vaughn that he and the man would bump heads if either moved suddenly. Vaughn spied on them in his soup spoon. Both Camden and Lady Millhauser had short hair and round glasses. They each wore black T-shirts with hand-painted slogans. Vaughn could not make out the slogans in his spoon. He was startled that people would be in T-shirts already, when here it was, still early spring. Last year at this time the snow was still falling. It had ruined the start of baseball for everyone (baseball, as Vaughn well knew, was a more evolved form of cricket that American people liked). But this winter had been exceptionally mild. Intriguingly, such seasonal variances were no longer accepted as natural. They were instead welcome fodder for psychotics and paranoiacs—ozone holes, el niño, weather tyrants, climate sabotage, melting ice caps—commuters were daily receiving updated bulletins on these topics from unfortunates camped on subway platforms with bullhorns, who found converts everywhere even as they linked these phenomena to the identifying magnetic strip found on Metrocards or the imminent CIA supervision of the EZ-Pass.

"Excuse me," said Camden to Vaughn. He was asking for more room in order to stand up. Vaughn apologized and, rising swiftly, shoved in his chair. Camden sidled through, flashed a kind smile, presumably off to make a phone call, perhaps to check his voice-mail, or to use the bathroom.

Vaughn liked to tour the lives of others, imagining himself included in their most mundane choices and responses because somehow, somewhere, someway, in this world of billions he'd ended up alone. All his friends in the city, none returned his telephone calls anymore. It had been months. His mail had fallen off. From the moment he arrived home, turning the key in his box to find nothing but HAVE YOU SEEN ME cards addressed to "Occupant" from "The National Center of Missing Citizens," all hope died, his mind stopped, his chest ached. He paused for many minutes to study today's photos of kidnapped folks, their dates of birth, dates of disappearance, feeling forgotten, standing there like something that'd been frozen in an upright posture in the vestibule. It burned every calorie to lug his heavy, hurting body up those five flights to his apartment, to bother with the turning on of a light, to cross the stupid room and check his answering machine—nope, no calls, never a blinking light, had he accidentally left it unplugged, should he check to see, had it broke, no, it still worked fine, it's just nobody cared about him—and admit the prospect of yet another night in his tiny East Village kitchenette, comforted by the blather of cable TV and the fake butter of pre-flavored microwave popcorn. *Have you seen me?* The only other choices were the dog run, the Indian restaurant, or possibly some riding about on the subway.

Camden rejoined Lady Millhauser. Their amusing banter immediately began anew. Vaughn let out a satisfied sigh. He liked these two. With their comradely presence so near, his rogan josh was even more sumptuous than usual. He continued to eavesdrop and to spot them occasionally in his fork, his licked-clean knife, or in the reflection of bent, dangling foil ribbons. They were not far behind him when he left the restaurant. Vaughn had fun imagining that they were following him and not the other way around. *Let's trail that longhair*, they were gamely whispering to one another. *Just for fun, let's see where he ends up.* Vaughn strolled east a few blocks, glanced over his shoulder. The couple had fallen several yards back but persisted in going his way. He turned up Avenue A. They did, too! Vaughn slowed to peruse the 70's T-shirt decals hung high in a shop window. Camden and Lady swerved around and passed him. They appeared not to notice Vaughn watching. They *pretended* to be engrossed in conversation; well, okay, perhaps they were not pretending, no doubt a conversation was a quite engrossing thing to have. They continued up A, past the hip coffee shop, the

Ukrainian restaurant, the overpriced burrito spot, the handmade ice cream place, and took a sudden left amongst a great many garbage pails to enter a building. *Why were they heading up to their apartment, so soon, so early? Was this an illicit relationship? But no,* he realized as he drew closer. He'd gotten it wrong. They had not stepped into an apartment foyer but into that music club above Tenth Street. What was its name, Blackie's, Whitey's, something like that? Vaughn stood beside the inevitable stick insect woman. Innumerable taped-up posters of rail-thin pop stars overlapped one another across the club's facade. There was a handwritten note to advertise tonight's gig—The Botswanas, Chrome Cranks, The Fall—three nobodies. Vaughn shrugged. Could be fun, who could say? He followed the couple inside.

ONCE IN BROWNIE'S, Lady Millhauser became astonished by the many hundreds of people attending a Tuesday night gig, and standing contentedly in a tiny room that stank like locker rooms and dried barf. "Who," she wondered aloud, "are all these people?" And don't they have to go to work tomorrow, she nearly added.

"Let's see," Camden smirked. Taped music blared over the Brownie's sound system; he had to raise his sarcasm up a few notches to make himself heard. "Over there are at least three men who are right wing—I'm talking about the buzz-cut jarheads in slacks, the ones with aviator glasses—and they like The Fall because, you see, they strongly believe that Mark E Smith is right wing. Fortunately, they do not concern us here."

At a small table beside the pinball machine, the waitress stood befuddled. "So," she was saying, "basically you want a banana daiquiri with no alcohol?"

"Very good," Brandon said. "And a protein element… it smells like bad cottage cheese or rotten eggs in this place, maybe you could put some of that in a blender, along with some kind of fiber, that's the important part here… like maybe some bran? You got bran?"

"Uh. Saltines?"

Clarke disrupted their negotiations long enough to order himself a double whiskey.

"And there stands a woman," Camden was telling Lady, "who is in love with Mark E Smith because she thinks he's hunky. And over there are some people who follow The Fall around… well, because it is better than doing nothing."

"Hi!" Betsy had almost entered the club. She spoke to the long-haired man in line behind her. His nose was wide, his deep brown eyes set far apart. His forehead bore a large, prominent mole.

"Uh," he responded with trepidation, "how d'you do?"

"Welcome to Brownie's," interrupted the doorman, wearing tattoos and a T-shirt two sizes too small.

"Can I ask something?" Betsy turned to the doorman. "Do you smell that, what is that? Is there a carcass inside?"

"Mold. Mildew. I don't know. Show me some ID and eight dollars. You can find out for yourself."

"And," Camden had just retrieved drinks from the bar. He handed Lady Millhauser her soda pop, then motioned with his own vodka tonic. "Tending bar tonight is a man who wants to be the most ill-mannered man in the world and therefore admires Mark E Smith… and over there, ah shit. There's Snook. Let's go nearer the stage."

"Right." Lady was surprised to see Snook. This meant that he had voyaged beyond his famously cramped apartment in East Orange, had momentarily opened the curtains and set aside his cloistered life of Fall calculations. There had been a time previous, when Snook was a brilliant young mathematician, that both she and Camden had grown acquainted with him. As a Fall know-it-all, he was a very popular party guest. He was into "solving" The Fall's numerological aspects. People would ply him with liquor and then ask him to explain his favorite band using a great big chart and a hunk of cheese. He was very obliging. Now he was just another agoraphobic, web-based hermit.

The doorman shone a flashlight on Betsy's out-of-state license. His biceps were enormous.

After the guy paid for the vodka tonic and soda pop, Colin moved up to the bar. "What's your selection of ale?" he inquired. "Have you anything like… Buckley's? Felinfoel? Bullmastiff?"

The bartender frowned at Colin but didn't respond.

"Oh, what about… Do you have any Brains?"

"You calling me stupid, you foreigner? You're the one." The bartender appeared mad. "You talk stupid, you know that? What kind of shittin' accent is that, anyway?"

Betsy checked her watch. "What time does The Fall go on?" she asked the doorman.

"When does the fall begin?" he sniggered. He handed back her license. "That's like a metaphysical question, ha, ha. They're next. Let's see." He checked a paper taped to the wall. "The Fall." He looked up at a clock. "Oh, soon."

"How soon?"

"Well… Pretty soon. It really depends upon your conception of time. Some insist that time is an illusion, that we are nothing but little patches of consciousness locked in many eternal Nows."

"You're rude," the long-haired mole-man spoke up from back of Betsy.

The doorman shrugged.

"Can I get you anything from the bar?" the waitress inquired of the smelly hippie gent with the chipped fingernail polish who stood in the middle of the swarm.

"From the bar. Yessssss," he hissed softly at last, "what do you have... in the way of cheese?"

"I'm sorry. 'Cheese,' did you say?"

"Yes." He looked dazedly about. "Is it available by the hunk?"

Two men in unusual reflective garments were intervening on Colin's behalf.

"He's from the United Kingdom," a man with a scruffy black beard explained to the bartender.

The cold-eyed man, who sat beside the bearded one, agreed. "It's not his fault."

"Just give him a Bass," nodded the first man.

The bartender snorted but fetched the drink.

"Thanks," said Colin.

"No problem," said the second man. "I have a soft spot for you barbarians."

Colin bit his tongue. He took his Bass, paid, and moved to the front of the room. Doubtless, he should feel lucky.

"Excuse me," Camden spoke up.

"Yes."

"I couldn't help but notice you talking... are you Welsh?"

"Yep."

"Great!" said Camden. "Check this out." He positioned himself under better lighting and

pointed at his T-shirt. It said, DUW DAMNIO Y
GYMRAEG PEDDANDAITH.

Colin had no response. He swigged his Bass; it
was cold; he winced.

"Get it?" Camden asked.

"Not exactly."

"Can't you read Welsh?"

"Sorry."

"Oh, man! It says, 'Goddamn the Pedantic
Welsh.' You know. A Fall quote."

"Of course, of course. Very cool. I'm rather
embarrassed to not know that. I should know how
to read Welsh."

"It's okay. Here," Camden pulled a small
container from his front pants pocket. "Want
some?"

"I don't think so. What have you got?"

"Amyl nitrate. From the West Village." He
uncapped the vial and held the inky pungence to
his nostrils. "Makes you… ahhhh." He staggered a
little as his blood pressure was reduced and heart
rate accelerated. He sounded suddenly quite dull-
witted. "Oh, sweet. So sweet. Here. Try."

"No. Thanks."

"Suit yourself," Camden shrugged, "you're the
boy laboring beneath the British yoke." Colin
snapped him a sharp look but Camden laughed
good-naturedly. "Just kidding with you." He
slapped Colin on the back. "You heard what
happened in New York the other week when The

Fall played Coney Island High?"

"No," Colin answered.

"Oh!" A clean-cut lad leaned in amongst them. Apparently, he'd been eavesdropping. "I read an awesome review in the *New York Times*." He wore an NYU shirt and off-white chinos. "I mean, the review was a pan, but everything it said just made my mouth water."

"Yeah," breathed the slender woman at his side, a peroxide blonde with green eyes that were flecked with lively bits of loose color. "We wished so much we could've seen it. We had to come tonight." Clutched to her heaving bosom was a late edition *New York Post* bearing the headline, BONES OF LOUIS ARMSTRONG FOUND ON MOON!

"Smith had a black eye," Camden explained to Colin. "He was missing some teeth."

Lady Millhauser winced. "The band fought before the gig."

Brandon watched in judgment as Clarke downed his double whiskey and ordered another. "C'mon!" Brandon finally yapped, his thumb moving in the direction of the stage. "We're going up." In dutiful accompaniment, Clarke rose to push a path through the throng for his short boss.

"I heard," said Camden, "something about Mark Smith chasing them around the hotel room, stripped to the waist. I believe he was twirling tassels on his nipples. Maybe he was yelling, 'Look what I can do!'"

"No," the clean-cut lad scowled, "I heard his girlfriend clocked him in the head with a telephone."

His slender date nodded. "That's what I heard, yeah."

"Smith's got a girlfriend?" asked Camden.

"Yeah, the keyboard chick," said the date. "Julia Nagle. That's his girlfriend."

"Oh."

"And I'm *so* not surprised to hear this is happening."

"Why?" asked Lady Millhauser, dreading the answer.

"Oh, you know," she said, with casual cattiness, "Smith's health is so *awful*. He's been told to give up drinking long ago. He's basically near-death."

At the bar, Hopper and Fredericks feigned drinking.

"This is not what we were told would occur," said Hopper.

"No," Fredericks agreed, looking in vain for instructions to appear upon the screen of his miniature apparatus.

"Should we be concerned?"

"Oh yes."

Hopper kept a close eye on Clarke while Fredericks snuck furtive glances at Vaughn, who now sat on the pinball machine in back, chatting with a woman in a red scarf.

"How is it they haven't seen each other?"

"Can't explain it. But this isn't good. This is against the plan. It is a predicament. Could be we've targeted the wrong interloper."

"It'll all be fine, I'm sure."

Vaughn found himself unable to follow any of Betsy's nervous blather. He faced her with an expression of devout attention while surveying the rest of the audience. It appeared Fall fans were all white, but for a group of scowling Asians with yellow backpacks and dyed hair. He saw at least one musician who'd come straight from rehearsal, her instrument zippered into a soft vinyl bag which she wore strapped about one shoulder. As they waited for the next band, several crowd members read paperbacks. Others wore headphones and listened to Discmans. A few were dressed in lycra. Most of the men needed to trim their sideburns.

Just then the lights dimmed and the pre-recorded music faded from the sound system. Tommy Crooks, The Fall's guitarist, came out first. Bassist Steve Hanley next appeared, strapping on his instrument. The drummer, Karl Burns, climbed behind his kit. Everyone not holding a bottle, a smoke, or a vial of amyl nitrate applauded. The rest whistled. "I recognize the balding bassist," Betsy told Vaughn, "and the drummer with the nose. They were in the band when I saw The Fall back whenever that was. But not this guitarist. And not that woman on the keyboards."

Vaughn acknowledged this with a small toss of his head.

Hanley rolled up his sleeves. The guitarist checked his tuning. The drummer loosened up the kick. The bassist nodded, drummer Burns clicked his sticks together four times. The song began with a bass slide and a lumbering beat.

"Wanna go up front?" Betsy asked Vaughn.

"Nah. You go ahead."

Betsy's expression did not change, though her behavior betrayed clear disappointment. Bidding farewell, she wandered off. Vaughn watched her slump forward, checking her watch repeatedly until she disappeared from his view.

"'Powderkeg,'" Colin was shouting at Camden. "This song's alright."

Crooks strummed his guitar without fingering any chords.

It's all fuzz and mid-range, thought Clarke. *An ungenerous room, no crack or snap.*

A pale man with an oddly swollen face appeared among the musicians. He walked onstage as if emerging from some sort of booth that induces premature aging. His hair looked patchy and his pallor was off. Carrying a lit cigarette, he advanced on the audience, braying something both sharp and indistinct.

"Hey," Colin cupped his hands around Camden's ear. Camden felt the Welshman spitting as he shouted. "Maybe you can tell me—what's

74

with the decrepit hippie wearing nail polish and chewing gum back there to the left of us?"

"Know him?" Camden yelled back.

"Should I? He appears to be stinking up the whole place."

"Yeah, he reeks."

"Reminds me of the low tide. As in, brackish mud. Rot. Nutrients."

"That's Alvin Snook."

"My god. That's Snook?"

"Uh-huh. Know him?"

"I think so." Colin was remembering Sweet Alicia's fascination with his website. "I think I hate him."

"Snook's pretty sad. A grad school burnout." Camden shrugged, then resumed yelling. "It happens. He was trying to define The Fall through arithmetic. After a decade or so, he announced that no one could work out what The Fall was, only what it was not. His conclusion was that The Fall could exist even if there were nobody in it." Camden waited for the song to quiet down a little. "Like," he eventually continued, "do you remember last year, in Belfast, when all the members dispersed? Snook believes that, in that brief period, The Fall still existed. It's just that there was nobody in it, you know? Because that was the way it was written up in music magazines; that, although the members have gone their separate ways, The Fall has not broken up. So that's pretty weird, right? But that's not all."

A few people bumped up against them, dancing. Colin sipped his Bass with a look of distaste while Camden went on. "Snook also believes—this is on his website but not a lot of people have made it into the section where this bit resides—he thinks that, for those few moments when The Fall existed with nobody in it, it went spindizzy about the world. Like some sort of prowling phantom, you know? It traveled around the globe, almost as a virus or something,[6] disrupting various musical personalities in which it did not belong."

"Oh, he sounds like a blast."

"Yeah," Camden drew another hit of amyl then offered it to everybody in the immediate vicinity. A few people agreeably inhaled the fumes of the vasodilator and, once appropriately faint, faces flushed, necks perspiring, passed back the vial. Camden turned back to Colin with his head lolled groggily. "Snook's got like, zero sense of humor, too. Talk to him. It's always a gas. Oh wait! Here he comes."

Mark E Smith had handed his half-gone cigarette to a short guy in the front row, a guy with studs in his eyelids and nostrils. Alvin Snook rushed forward, nearly tripping over a young man who had gone down on one knee to double-knot the laces of his bowling shoes. Whenever he left his apartment for an event such as this, Snook was in a frantic dash for souvenirs. He approached the short guy, offering him $5 — then $10 — then $15 ("SOLD!") — for the unsmoked portion of Smith's cigarette.

Upon the wall that abutted the stage, a spotlight cast a huge shadow of the drummer's head and of the narrow-billed cap that he wore. Lady Millhauser watched the silhouette lustily wallop a snare. Of all The Fall's drummers, Karl Burns had always been the sturdiest and the strongest. And now, he literally overshadowed the band.

The first awful song ended and Smith wobbled over to his shoulder bag at the foot of the drums. His sickliness disturbed Lady. From where she stood, directly in front of the guitarist, the singer's control of his most basic motor functions seemed precarious. " — Have a little discussion about what the set's gonna be," the singer spoke indistinctly, "or whether this set's gonna be all over…" Whatever he meant to say apparently displeased Hanley, who knocked about on his instrument in order to drown out the singer's mutterings. When that didn't succeed, and the singer remained audible, the bassist shouted disagreeably. Their bickering was broken up by a tinkling keyboard sample broadcast over the house sound system. It came out of the Roland Synthesizer being played on the other side of the stage by Julia Nagle, a curly-haired woman in a striped orange top.

Smith pawed through papers in his bag. "That's

right," he indicated his band members, "they're gonna beat me up like the big men that they are!" Much of the crowd, including the clean-cut lad and his date, roared in approval. The programmed musical intro segued into a thunderous rhythm. A woman in a red scarf near Lady Millhauser began to rock out enthusiastically. The bassist, bored, looked into the distance.

Brandon recognized this as the title song from their new CD. Earlier in the day, when he'd played it in his office, the words had reminded Brandon of last year's torturing of Levin's son, what he'd read of it in the noted tabloids, details about being bound by Harlem youths and repeatedly stabbed with a kitchen knife before being put out of his misery with a shot to the head, the beloved only offspring of the Time Warner CEO handled like some hated animal just to get him to reveal the PIN code to his ATM card. The music felt scattered, impatient, wild-eyed. But the lyrics had also reminded Brandon of suburban youths arrested by guns-in-your-face federales following said youths' successful hacking into the local branch bank's system to alter some rich baddie's account. This morning, the music had seemed so electric, so computer-driven, so unforgiving...

It was different now.

The keyboardist swayed timidly to the song's beat. Smith looked sluggish and preoccupied as he laid his jacket down upon the stage, picked it up, laid it down several more times. He groggily shuffled items about the stage, then knelt and smoked a cigarette. A tornado of electronic samples enclosed him.

"Less structure," Colin recommended, in a hearty voice.

Out of the corner of her eye, Lady Millhauser saw a waitress approach and scream, "Gin and Mountain Dew!" On Lady's other side, Betsy raised a hand. The waitress yelled an amount of money. Betsy passed money around Lady and received her drink.

Lady Millhauser smiled.

"Been a long time since I had one of these," Betsy shouted.

"They good?" asked Lady.

Betsy nodded eagerly and lent her the cup for a taste.

"Mmmmm," agreed Lady.

Without warning, the singer reached down and, perhaps accidentally, unplugged the bass guitar. Hanley stared helplessly. "The masquerade," Smith spoke into the mike without enthusiasm. He reconnected the bassist, then played around with the microphone cord. "Masqueraaaaaa." He collapsed one mike stand, and then another.

"A masquerade."

A bar tray floated over Clarke's head, bearing a double whiskey. He experienced a moment of stuporous panic. His mouth went dry as he imagined that this beverage had been dispatched down to him from the all-seers at Seagram's who lived in the sky. A hand and arm emerged, before the waitress to whom these belonged managed to position herself beside Clarke and request payment. Gratefully, Clarke poured the punishing refreshment down his parched throat. Seagram's was not alone in scaring him; The Fall had started to sound to him like Devo fronted by some maniac droner. Smith seemed to be singing full-volume though off-mike. "Evaporated," he appeared to say at one point. The singer raised his left hand in a half-clenched sort of palsied claw, then reached over to steal a few dissonant notes from Nagle's keyboards. "Maaaasssssk…"

In the back of the club, Vaughn overheard a couple of supermodels arguing. One, a redhead with a jeweled belt cinched about her wispy waist, had dashed her non-fat yogurt cone to the floor in outrage. "They almost killed me playing that number!" she was screeching as the song finished.

Their next song was also uptempo. Smith apparently recalled a lot more of the words. He seemed altogether engaged. He even looked at Nagle with something close to appreciation before passing the microphone into the audience. It ended up in the grasp of an ROTC cadet who held, in his other hand, a Macy's shopping bag.

"The cult of The Fall will never die until the stars come right again," the cadet belted in the

80

microphone, "We are beyond good and evil, beyond all but this eccentric human phonograph who left his heart in San Francisco." Smith gestured, encouraging the cadet to get more on the mike.

"Excuse me," Colin had retreated to the middle of the crowd, "aren't you Alvin Snook?"

"Indeed."

"Well, it's a pleasure to meet you. I know your website." He looked incredulously at the great Snook's face. Observed from close up, his head was so lumpy Colin could only speculate that Snook's mother, while pregnant, had been kicked in the belly by Geoff Hurst. "Perhaps you would be so kind as to educate me about this song."

"I will tell you everything about this piece, if such is your desire. It's entitled 'Everybody But Myself.' I know for a fact that Mark E Smith got up one morning and ate a biscuit before composing it. He did not eat toast, as many people believe, but a biscuit. It is not known what type of biscuit, but there are many theories."

"Interesting."

"Now, moving on, may I assume you're familiar with the song 'City Hobgoblins,' one of The Fall's earlier pieces?"

"Okay."

"Note how, accented in the title, comes the word 'hob,' as in 'HOBNOB,' a popular brand of biscuit in the United Kingdom. Perhaps this is

Mark E Smith's biscuit of choice; again, I reiterate, there are many theories. 'Nob,' the biscuit's lost syllable, is, significantly, British slang for 'penis.' 'Goblin,' of course, is how 'gobbling' would sound if pronounced by a working-class prole of Mark E Smith's ilk. I can therefore argue with resolute certainty that 'City Hobgoblins' is about oral sex."

"Huh. Never thought of that. But then again, words in most languages are made up of letters that can be rearranged to make other words. This means fuck all."

"Yes. Now pardon me, please. I must instigate a procurement of memorabilia."

By the time Mark Smith had walked to the front of the stage and bent down in order to retrieve his old microphone from the ROTC cadet, Alvin Snook had already bought it up. Smith straightened up and backed groggily into the guitarist, who shoved him away in anger.

Meanwhile, the band grimly played on. To Clarke, they all seemed to be contemplating retirement. The synthesizer was stuck on one maddening loop. *Can they find the plug on that thing?* Clarke wondered. *Somebody should pull the plug.* The singer hollered unintelligibly in the background, as might a man being driven mad by machines. Clarke was reminded of the climax in an anti-technology filmstrip, when molten metal filled the veins of human slaves.

Clarke suddenly felt very... *strange.* The many

warming whiskeys, his boss's head-spinning, heart-breaking betrayal, this musical torture. What he really needed, he knew in a flash, was a serving of eKstaZi—"the e" as it was heralded—an endocrine stimulant which, once ingested, would lift him on wings of bliss to soar over and past this mean, dank terrain... He looked about desperately but Brownie's was an establishment that attracted neither drug-peddlers nor legions of experiment-minded teens. The clientele here would rather plumb real-life misery than welcome the far-out travels of one's most exceptional soul.

Without warning, Clarke's stomach turned over. His palms itched, felt prickly, his tongue wrong somehow, engorged. His knees went watery and a clammy sweat broke across his brow. He clenched his throat against an eruption of puke, as frantically he sought out the restroom. He located it to the side of the stage and fairly flung himself into its single stall just as he lost control and heaved up everything: Frog, The Fall, Fredericks, Hopper, and—most of all—Brandon, whose treachery had provided such valuable instruction until tonight when, in the face of the Seagram's deal, it had turned upon Clarke himself.

Colin felt a twitch in the pocket of his dufflecoat. The skull had begun to heat up. Pan was up to no good.

Smith had discovered another microphone on the stage and was using it to scratch his back.

A little, pug-nosed, pig-tailed cutie pie, standing in stacked heels, was incensed. "Play your hits," she ordered the band, with considerable insistence, "you bastards!"

The bassist looked at her in amusement.

"No!" Colin over-rode the cutie pie, in a shout. "Do the three rules of audience!"

"No," Snook screamed over Colin, "do the introduction to the John the Postman twelve inch of 'Louie, Louie!'"

All requests were ignored as, rather begrudgingly, another song began. Each player remained isolated from the rest. But for brief eye contact with the bassist, the band did not acknowledge one another.

Camden slipped between the clean-cut lad and his slender date, stepped around the pig-tailed cutie pie, and shouldered aside the ROTC cadet, that he might join Colin and Snook.

"How'd it go?" Colin asked. He explained to Snook how Camden had hit upon the ingenious notion that The Fall would perform much better if Mark Smith were annoyed in some way. To inspire a blistering performance from an enraged Smith, Camden had gone up to shout at his girlfriend, the keyboardist: "Show us yer cunt, Julia!"

"I see," said Snook, middle-class lip curling in disdain. "And what happened?"

"Oh, I don't think she heard me. And the people on either side of me didn't grasp the

84

import of what I was attempting. They gave me filthy looks."

"So," said Colin. "You buggered off a bit sharpish, eh?"

"Yes."

They watched Mark Smith kneel and remove papers from his shoulder bag. He did this for several minutes, singing only occasionally. The song wound down and gradually stopped. Nobody much applauded.

Snook sputtered a bit of spit down his chin before succeeding in blowing a bubble with his gum. "Sorry," said Snook. "Have we met before?"

"Yes," said Camden, bemused. "I'm, uh. Smith."

"Ah. Smith. How interesting. No doubt you know, in Onomancy, that Smith is the NAME OF CLANDESTINE CONSPIRACY THEORIES. Citizen Wolfie Smith. Winston Smith in *1984*. Dr Zachary Smith of *Lost In Space* — "

"He of hiding behind girls."

"Morrissey of The Smiths — "

"Who sang, '*The people in the graveyard/They're all dead/It's quite simply not fair/I wish it was me instead/Every day I awake and think of sex/Interminable rainy Sundays, exams, and stuff like that*' to insecure virgins in a theatre beside McDonald's on the Reeperbahn."

Snook persevered. "Mr and Mrs Smith. And of course, *Alias Smith and Jones*."

Camden had no more smart-ass retorts.

"As for Mark Smith," Snook began.

"Mark," Colin finished for him. "Is the name of 'I couldn't be arsed to think of a proper name, that'll do.'"

"I like your shirt," Betsy told Lady Millhauser. It said, CALIFORNIANS ONLY THINK OF SEX.

"Oh," Lady blushed. "Thanks. It's a Fall quote." She gestured in Camden's direction. "He made me wear it."

"Your boyfriend?"

"Him? God, no. Just a friend."

The drummer initiated a new song with a soft patter on his crash cymbal. Smith kept going through papers, distractedly organizing his bag. He found a paper and, clutching it, rose unsteadily, ambling crookedly to the front of the stage. Someone in the audience handed him a beer. Smith took it in exchange for the mike, which got passed around the front row. It ended up with Brandon.

"Here's the thing," Brandon hollered into the microphone, "here's why, as I study you fucks, I remain underenthused. Okay, I'm thinking, so maybe I can get them a royalty of 13%, less a 10% packaging deduction; but who're we going to hook them up with in the studio? The cocksucker I'd want, he's worth one hundred and fifty G's and three points. No fucking chance. Maybe we could get some hot-shit whiz kid to remix them for four grand a track plus two points. And yet..."

A woman nearby wormed the microphone out of his grip. Brandon plunged a thumb deep into her eye socket and retook the mike. "I look at you," he proceeded to tell The Fall from the floor of Brownie's, "and I think: fuck, they're old. They dress like shit."

Smith took a microphone from the drumkit. He picked up his jacket once more, and this time he laid it upon Nagle's synthesizer. He began to pound the keyboard through his jacket, as someone might blanket a block of ice before hammering at it.

And still, Brandon would not relent. "I'm thinking, I'd have to call in favors, get someone to write material for these fuckheads, get some dipshit bombshell to come sing vocals. I'm thinking, making a sexy video out of those decrepit English bodies takes a lot of make-up and crew. All this, you see, costs! MONEY, MONEY, MONEY, MONEY, MONEY. I'm thinking about a tour gross income that doesn't offset the hassle of dealing with English fucks."

Smith smirked strangely and stopped pounding on the synthesizer just long enough to see the tattooed doorman descend on Brandon and bearhug him straight out of the building. The last thing anybody made out was something the label head howled about T-shirt sales.

The crowd erupted in applause and The Fall hit an excited groove. Betsy gyrated about and hooted. Lady nonchalantly ran one of her Mary Janes along the floor to scrap something sticky off the sole, thinking, *Shape us into a mob and plainly our IQ plummets.* Smith stood up there, scratching his nose and neck. The singer seemed to have nothing to add. He pulled off the woolly stretched-out crewneck that hung from his skinny frame, revealing a polyester shirt that resembled wet plastic in the stage lights. His shirt was tucked in, making his underfed condition apparent. He pounded again upon Nagle's instrument, then drifted offstage. The song ended.

"What do you make of that song?" Betsy asked Lady.

Lady Millhauser was noncommittal. "I've probably sat two thousand times listening to that record and trying to make sense of it and what do I have now but a lot of memories of different rooms in which I sat listening, trying to make sense out of it. I don't know." She clenched her shoulders and raised them in a shrug. "I could speak about the rooms, certainly."

"You know," Colin was teasing Snook, "I have this recurring dream in which I'm invited to The Fall's hotel suite in order to read from your dissertation, *Neighbourhood Of Infinity: Mark E Smith From Within An Hegelian Marxist Dialectic.*"

"Yes," Snook seemed to smile. "I am most especially proud of that 'an' in the title, of course."

88

"So Smith listens to your dissertation for a bit…" Colin paused.

"Yes?"

"Oh, then a unicorn enters…"

"AND?"

"The unicorn is holding a teeny-tiny origami model of the hotel… "

Snook's voice was frantic. "Did you *ever* find out if Mark E Smith *really* was coming from within an Hegelian Marxist dialectic?"

"Well, no." Colin didn't have a clue what an Hegelian Marxist dialectic was. They didn't have them where he came from. "Y'see, I always wake up too soon."

Snook clawed at his own face in agitation.

Inside the locked toilet stall, Clarke lay sprawled upon the filthy tile groaning. He was alone, on his back, in the bathroom. He looked up at cobwebs and corroded pipes and, in the top-most corner of the ceiling, a felt-penned haiku that said,

Dave Datblygu's dad says
There's only one drummer
And that's Ringo.

He raised his head to spit into the bowl, swiped weakly at his mouth with a sheet of tissue, then flushed once more. Brandon's amplified words were audible via throbbing shudders in the floor that climbed directly into his cerebellum.

After a time, clatter erupted on the other side of

Clarke's toilet stall. He could hear the sink and towel dispenser being knocked upon and it sounded as if someone were scrambling to get free from the trash can. Clarke scooted up the wall to peep through a crack in the stall.

The bathroom door squeaked open.

Musical racket poured in.

His friend Vaughn stood framed in the doorway. But Vaughn did not see Clarke—all of Vaughn's attention was focused upon a woman who, just then, trailed cigarette butts and crumbled-up towels as she staggered out of the garbage.

Abruptly, Vaughn apologized to her. He leaned out, glancing backward to confirm that this was, indeed, signed as the men's bathroom.

The woman motioned for Vaughn to return inside. She started to say something. She lost her balance. Vaughn caught her. Clarke could see that she wore her hair in tightly wound golden curls. She looked up at Vaughn with worried blue eyes.

"My god." Vaughn muttered. "You're burning up." He freed one hand, wetted some paper towels, and began to mop her forehead. She slouched against the wall, appearing somewhat comforted by Vaughn's ministrations. Her elbow slid relaxedly and hit a handle which caused the urinal to flush.

"It's not what you think," she moaned.

From where he lay, Clarke strained to make out what she was saying.

"It's... you think."

He was losing many of her words beneath The Fall's maniacal thundering. He recognized the woman's unusual clothes—the reflective fabric that rustled like crepe paper—as those favored by Fredericks and Hopper.

"Listen," she told Vaughn, trying mightily to push off from the wall and stand on her own. "We have no... You must give me the..."

...*The what?* Clarke couldn't tell what she'd said. He closed his eyes, hoping it would help him hear her better.

"Uh..." Vaughn sounded uneasy. "You must mean someone else. I'm terribly sorry."

"Vaughn," she continued, short of breath. "Trust me... The continuum pirates... weakened you with a cage of friendlessness. It's their weapon. You received the... Pan tonight. They've dispatched pirates to intercept it."

Clarke had never seen his friend look so stunned. "Pan" clearly meant something to Vaughn, he could see that.

"Come, come," the woman went on, sounding stronger every second. "It started with the unearthing of a skull in Caerleon—"

"Hunh." Vaughn appeared still more nervous. He forced a snort of laughter. "Not me. I mean, I do work at the Institute. I deal with those sorts of artifacts, ruins, within my division. The archeology division. But you have the wrong guy. Do you...

Could you have me confused with one of my co-workers?"

"You don't understand." She cast him a tender look. "I'm from another continuum, another QST altogether. There aren't *mistakes* once you can straddle QSTS. Things get checked and re-checked."

This time Clarke was positive he had gotten all her words but he still felt something move in, a deep shadow of some sort, to obscure the woman's precise meaning. He was thankful when he heard Vaughn ask, "What are you saying?"

"What do you think? You think you know of life, here in this New York, in this America. You are *greatly mistaken*. Oh, would that it were so simple!" The woman was speaking louder now, choking back tears. Her features had grown dark. "Vaughn! It is a stranger, a more terrible world than you can ever possibly imagine! What you call 'existence'" — she swept her arm — "is only a small part of being alive."

Again, Clarke felt sure he would vomit. This time it traveled from his head downward, rather than vice versa. This was the precise opposite of a glorious journey fueled by the e. A most vivid presentment of evil — inexplicable, unimaginable evil — expressed itself to him. Something like a poisonous cloud filled the room, choking him. "Vaughn… " Clarke tried to call out to his friend but found little air left in his lungs. His voice was a whisper. "...Vaughn." As with earlier in the day, when he'd met Fredericks and Hopper, Clarke now grappled with a sudden sense of the unspeakable, a terror which inhabited only his unconscious and presented itself as a sensation of profound discomfort rather than something which the mind might diagnose. He drew himself inward, redoubling attempts to unite those splintered bits of himself which lay scattered about the bathroom floor. Panting with considerable effort, he managed to lift himself onto the toilet, where at last he sat, head bowed. He inhaled deeply through his nose and briefly regained stability. Vaughn and the woman kept speaking.

"I want to call you... 'Helen.'" Vaughn spoke with low intensity. "Is this your name? Helen?"

"Yes."

"Do I know you?"

"You remember *something* but you... don't know what?"

"Yeah."

"Like déjà vu?"

"Yeah, or... like recalling the subject of an old dream. All of this seems... familiar." Vaughn shuddered. "There's a... recognition, a sense of belonging." He patted his chest. "In here. A remembrance. I seem to already know you though I cannot place you."

"The word for that," Helen said softly, "is

haunted. You feel *haunted* by me."

"But it's more, it's... I love you. Do you know? I love you but... *but who are you?* Where did you come from?"

"I'm from another QST. But I guess..." She coughed raspily, laughingly indicated her wobbly condition and feverish brow. "I guess I just wasn't made for these times."

"What's that, a QST?"

"It's... oh, that's difficult. How to explain? I'll tell you this way: in my QST, the all-time biggest-selling recording is by a painter in this QST whom you call Don Van Vliet."

Clarke was almost jolted off his toilet. He struggled against dwindling strength as he clung to the woman's every word.

"It's named *Trout Mask Replica,*" Helen continued, "and it's recorded under the pseudonym Captain Beefheart—"

"And His Magic Band, yes, I know. We've got that here. It's from 1969. Not a lot of people own it, but I do. It's very good."

"Yes."

"It might be my favorite record."

"Okay. Well, try to conceptualize this, darling—in your QST, *Trout Mask Replica* has actually sold ninety-six million more units than any other single recording. Which is to say, *it's the all-time biggest-seller in this QST also.* But here, a variety of interactions on the submolecular level allow the industry to successfully hush this up, so the event carries no resonance. In every QST, the sales figures of *Trout Mask Replica* are the very same. But in my QST, people are cognizant of it. Resonance and cognizance are the only ways in which parallel continuums differ. You see?"

Clarke felt himself fading from consciousness. He wouldn't be awake very much longer.

"So," Vaughn said, "the music's better where you're from?"

"I wish that were so." Clarke now heard Helen dimly through a thickening haze. "No, the music's exactly the same… Our cultures create precisely the same works of art… In my QST, he's more celebrated as Captain Beefheart; in this QST, he's more celebrated as Don Van Vliet… That's the difference."

These were the last words which reached Clarke's consciousness before he drifted away. His body slumped on the toilet. His head settled against the stall. The corners of his mouth drew up and small crow's feet crinkled in the corners of his closed eyes as peacefully, through the smile of an infant, he slumbered.

The start of another song drew Mark Smith back onto the Brownie's stage, but, rather than sing, Smith rolled up his sleeves, one at a time. He pulled up his pants. He tucked in his shirt. He put his hands in his pockets. Oddly exasperated, Smith gesticulated at Burns, the drummer. He appeared to want the drummer to rush the beat. He hovered above the pouch in which Burns kept his extra drumsticks. Inexplicably, Smith grabbed up the sticks and tossed them offstage (these discarded drumsticks presently can be observed in THE PERMANENT COLLECTION OF ALVIN SNOOK).

Furious, Burns leapt at Smith and threw him across the stage. Everything was knocked about. The synthesizer was upset. A mike stand was toppled. Smith cowered behind the bassist. The musicians had ceased to play but the song went on, for a drum track continued to pound from the synthesizer. The drummer shouted in Smith's face. The bassist worked to keep them separated. "Get over there," Hanley screamed, ordering Burns back to his kit.

The audience applauded madly.

"Speech!" Betsy hollered. "Speech!"

Rather than return to his drumkit, the drummer tidied up the stage. Nagle tried to straighten out the mikes. The bassist and guitarist started again to play. They seemed to think there was still a song.

The music was so loud it shook the silver earrings that dangled from Lady Millhauser's ears. She was beyond disappointed, far beyond. She had come for musical enlightenment, not this, this... this piece of performance art from a sociopath. She could barely recognize herself in such an environment. "I feel that we should leave for a moment," she murmured to Betsy, "in order to give the band some time in which to regain their composure."

Betsy looked as if she might laugh. Instead she turned and, quizzically, searched Lady's eyes. She found something there that she had not quite expected. On an impulse, Betsy wrapped her arms about Lady Millhauser and drew her into a protective embrace. "That's awfully sweet," Betsy blushed, and meant by this a great deal more.

Smith was holding his jacket again. He snuck across the stage and slapped rather dodgily at the strings on the guitarist's instrument. Crooks shoved him hard into Hanley.

"Big words add to any disgrace!" a chubby yuppie in a green turtleneck shrieked behind Lady Millhauser.

Camden, who now held Brandon's microphone, remembered something: he hadn't become a Fall fan until he'd learned to revile drum machines and synthesizers and the like; The Fall had been the only band he could think of that seemed to revile those technologies as much as he. Camden's revulsion had, at its core, a single incident. Some years before, he had innocently composed a piece of music on the family computer. He had been very pleased with this piece of music, as it had sounded pretty much like that "scratty" music that was coming out of England at the time. He had invited his parents to listen to it, and they'd said,

"Very nice, dear," in that way that only parents have of saying, "Very nice, dear." He had invited his friends to listen to it, but they'd been more impressed with the computer itself than with Camden's composition. He had invited Trudy Turnbull around, when his parents were away (she had wanted sex with him, and Camden had never done sex before). And Camden had felt it a good idea to have his first sex with Tracy Turnbull right there on the living room carpet, with his composition blaring out, all fake crashy drums and throbbies and burbles...

So he and Tracy had begun, and... and... just when he was almost there, just when he was hurtling down the rabbit hole and catching sight of the Mad Hatter...

Tracy Turnbull had spoken up, in the voice of some cruel Queen of Hearts, "What is this shit?" She stood, stormed over to the computer, and depressed the power button. A dreadful quiet descended and then Camden—a portrait of rigid arousal lying there on the living room carpet—distantly heard Tracy's guffaw as she put her pants back on and left.

When Camden next passed her in the school corridor there was nothing but icy silence before Tracy's friends nudged each other and started to giggle.

Subsequently, Camden reviled drum machines and synthesizers and the like, and admired, or thought he admired, The Fall…

In the disarray, Smith had retreated behind Nagle. Suddenly livid, Camden was inspired to speak. "Yo!" He yelled in the microphone. He relished hearing his voice echo about Brownie's. It felt good. "Fuckin' play! NONE OF THIS GIMMICK SHIT. This is a fuckin' gimmick! Fuckin' play!" Nagle looked at him, then checked nervously behind her. She saw Smith standing there and was reassured. "This is a gimmick! ARE YOU THE FALL? OR ARE YOU A GIMMICK?" Nagle smiled tightly and nodded at Camden. "Don't gimme this gimmick shit," he pointed at Burns, "fuckin' play! YOU!" Smith advanced to the front of the stage, peaceably carrying yet another microphone behind his back. The ROTC cadet and his jarhead pals were pushing Camden this way and that, attempting to wrestle the microphone away from him. "GET BEHIND THE DRUMS AND FUCKIN' PLAY!" Camden hollered.

People applauded as Burns dispiritedly retook his drum stool. The bassist still played. The voice of the soundman surfaced over Brownie's house speakers. "Everybody," he said, in a bored tone, "just shut the fuck up. Just shut the fuck up. Everybody shut the fuck up."

The short guy from before reached up to pat Smith on the leg and muttered, "Wonderful, eh?"

Someone near Betsy passed Crooks a beer. The guitarist took a sip and returned it. He then sought to defend himself. "I can't play my guitar," Crooks explained, stooping to speak into the short microphone on his amplifier, "when he broke my fucking string."

Applause.

"That guy," Smith instantly retorted, "is a Scottish man. And there's a fucking animal on drums. Fucking idiot." Burns shouted as Smith continued, "I've been assaulted in public here by two people. Or three people. You've been witness to it. I'll tell you what. These three—I got attacked, see? Some fucker pulled a gun out on me. From fucking Pakistan or somewhere. These three walked out on me! In the fucking dressing room! *As usual.*" Hanley and Burns rolled their eyes at Smith. Lacking microphones, they clattered on their instruments to drown him out. "It's very hard when we're together!" Smith declared finally and left the stage. The musicians conferred. They started another song.

"Is this," Hopper asked a man at the bar. "What a Fall gig is usually like?"

"Smith's pretty much inebriated all of the time," the man admitted, after giving it some thought. "I don't think he's got a thread of reality running through his life right now."

"And," Fredericks had to know. "Exactly who are you?"

"Me? Oh. I'm their tour manager."

After some shoving about, a sweaty Camden

returned to Colin's side. He was flushed with the sort of primal catharsis such idiotic antics provide.

Colin acknowledged him with a short nod. "Strange use of the microphone," he said lightly, "at least, you might have proclaimed a few things in rock and roll which should be banned."

Camden didn't follow. "Like what?"

"Oh, y'know. Acoustic guitars. And basses with the ends chopped off. The law should forbid them. And hairdressers, or anything attendant thereto. Oh and, most of all, rock stars doing loads of drugs, and then sobbing about it in public afterward when they happen to have a new album out after a major 'lull.'"

Camden found the idea intriguing. "Or what about people with English degrees writing lyrics?"

"Yep. Them too."

"You're right," Camden kicked his Keds in shame. "Had my chance and I blew it."

The drummer eyed Smith, who now hid backstage. The bassist and guitarist muttered kindly to each other as they played a wordless number. Nagle flipped through a book that rested upon her synthesizer. She stood oddly, with her hands down and chest held high, as if auditioning for a Broadway musical. There was scattered applause as good old reliable Hanley, the bassist, cued the end of the instrumental.

A pudgy, pasty background figure, Hanley had stuck it out through The Fall's often difficult dufflecoat years, their frightening and wonderful phase, their Kurious Leap Forward, their bent and sinister counter-reformation. For two decades, Hanley had labored unwashed beneath the intolerant tyrant's touch, being allowed little leeway, made small to allow the master to loom large. *Yet*, Colin thought, *does not his instrument supply the base of it all, the throbbing heart of the band?* Even Snook would have to agree that if/when Hanley left the band, The Fall really would be kaput.

"Mark!" Betsy yelled. She squeezed Lady's hand. "C'mon back, Mark! Say you're sorry!"

In the men's restroom, Vaughn was interrogating the woman he loved. For if he knew *Trout Mask Replica*'s actual sales, he argued, then wasn't he now more of her QST than his own?

To stay with her was all that Vaughn desired. To be with Helen was to feel darkness retreat, the sun emerging from behind some obstacle, the heart recognizing a most trusted friend. When he gazed upon her, the change that crept across his soul was almost eerie. He had never fathomed just how lonely he had been before. He felt electrified by her nearness. His bones fairly thrummed with joy. He would do anything to hold onto this feeling. Could he return with her?

But it seemed that every answer she possessed was nonsense to him. The quantum syntax in this time and place, she said, was "utterly vulgar." She tapped her forehead with a fist, complained of a shortage of time. She kept asking for the thing, this head she needed, the head of Pan.

"I wish I had it," Vaughn moaned, "truly." He attempted to tear his gaze from her face but found that he could not. "I mean, all the archivists know the myth, of course. The Norse buried half of the Great God on the other side of the planet and the Celts held his head with Cymry somewhere in... I don't know, modern day Wales—"

"It's true!"

"No, no..." It took but an instant—an instant in which Vaughn's mind sailed through all he knew of Norse capabilities, charted cartographically—an instant which recalled the multitude of prehistoric legends which, in their core, cradled seeds of some actual occurrence, the oral histories regularly authenticated through new technologies—an instant in which he studied this woman he loved and wanted so—it took just an instant for Vaughn's skepticism to lift. "—*Oh my god!*"

"The body is here, Vaughn. Right here. In Manhattan. This was the other side of the planet back then. *Pan's torso is buried directly below us.*"

"*Jesus!*" He sniffed the air in suspicion. *Could that*, he speculated, *be what smells so of such sinister foulness?*

"Yes," Helen said, reading his mind.

"Who are these pirates?"

"Well, obviously, a great resurgence, a wave of primal power, awaits the people who piece Pan back together. These pirates, they're from a renegade continuum. I'm the QST officer who's been sent to intercept them but... something's, I don't know, I'm not usually made so ill. I haven't time. I must return. So you have got to give me what you have. You see, darling?"

"Yes."

"You really do not know what I am speaking about, do you?"

"No."

"Oh, my."

They stood for a time without talking.

Mark Smith had come back. He stooped and picked a mike up off the stage. As he sang the first line of "Lie Dream of a Casino Soul," he casually sidled up to Tommy Crooks and, to the surprise of all, swiped at the guitarist's face with the microphone cord.

The cord snapped a sharp swath down through the front row. It nearly whipped Lady Millhauser in the face. Camden quickly ducked. The vial of intoxicant flew from his grasp. Narrowly missing Betsy's sweater, the amyl nitrate instead splashed sickeningly across Lady's shirt. She squealed, spun, and immediately shoved her way to the door. "I smell like a mimeograph machine!" Lady Millhauser wailed as she plunged outside.

She stood on the corner of Tenth and A. She wiped her runny nose on the back of a hand, noticing then how awfully her skin stank of cigarettes. With nicotine skin and mimeograph shirt, she hated it here. Her pulse raced. Very swiftly, a storm gathered. She saw an unleashed collie relieving itself nearby, and averted her gaze. It was like that all the time in New York now, women without undergarments strolling past in skimpy clothes, couples making love with the lights on and the drapes thrown open. It was a city watched through arrested glances.

So too with this Fall show, which reminded her of walking into a convenience store and observing, there on the cashier's monitor, a pornographic motion picture; or of pupils in her classes who, when called upon to read aloud from their assignments, rhapsodized about graphic intimacies which mortified everyone, especially (eventually) the student. Softly, swiftly, Lady would interrupt their recitation, motion for them to retake their seat, and call on another, less emotive pupil.

She felt much the same discomfiture and unease when a sudden channel switch landed her, accidentally, on the television program *Cops*, a show she'd read was meticulously constructed from thousands of hours of surveillance tape, parsed to the action sequences and edited to remove the police abuse and vulgarity which was so indispensable to the cop arsenals. She could stand only a few moments of *Cops* before, flustered, she would leap hastily to unplug the whole damn appliance. The shirt-waisted drunkards, the sobbing spouses, the cuffed suspects, the cowering kiddies. Someone toppled in a pool of blood. A wobbly screwdriver thrust in blurry rage.

The lady blushed.

Why were such shows shown? Who deemed their necessity? Many termed it "reality" but was not a library also reality, or a letter in a window, a book by Arthur Machen? Not all things required viewers to be real. As far as she knew, they didn't broadcast triple bypasses or bathroom breaks, but nobody forgot their existence.

Helen and Vaughn embraced. "Darling," Helen squeezed his arm, "look for me here. That's one of the things so damnably wrong with this QST..." She leaned against his chest, talking quietly. "You still have to locate me."

"Where do—" but Vaughn was interrupted. The bathroom door flew open and there stood some movie star guy in a dufflecoat, tossing something between his hands.

"Coming through!" Colin yelled, slipping between them. "Step aside! Got a red-hot head of Pan here." He dashed to the bathroom sink and began to run cold water on the skull that had started literally to burn a hole in his pocket.

"Well…" Helen gave Vaughn a sad smile. "That explains that."

"Ahhhh," choked Vaughn.

They both looked at Colin. He had pumped liquid soap from the dispenser and now submerged the head of Pan in a fine lather.

"So this…" Vaughn sobbed openly. "Ah, goodbye."

"Find me," Helen whispered and kissed him. She stepped in back of Colin.

"Hey," Vaughn spoke through his tears. Colin looked up. "Do you mind?" Vaughn motioned him toward the bathroom corridor that led back to the club. "Can I see you out here a second?"

"Sure." He moved to drain the sink and towel off the skull. "Just a second."

"Leave it," Vaughn said, "it'll be okay. Just come out here, would you?"

Colin shrugged and stepped outside. The moment lingered, during which she looked across the bathroom at Vaughn in gratitude, before the door swung shut behind Colin, and Helen vanished.

"Yeah?" Colin asked, and immediately something like a bomb went off nearby. The building shuddered.

"Wha..?" asked Colin nervously. "Is it an earthquake?"

"Nah," Vaughn jabbed a finger at the club windows, "an electrical storm just broke out." He regained some measure of control. "I only wanted you to see."

"Oh. Yeah. Cool. Thanks."

"Hi," Betsy had come outside to see if Lady was okay beneath the lightning. "Thought I'd check up on you."

"Thanks," said Lady, "guess I'm a wimp."

"Not at all."

"What did I miss?"

"Oh. Let's see. The highlight was the keyboardist. She removed her top. She was wearing, underneath, a sports bra. Looked very emaciated, though. Other than that, the guitarist kicked at the singer. The singer yelled and slapped at him. The guitarist flipped him off. The singer picked his nose... he scrounged about on the floor for a while, and then he came up with a cigarette. So then they end the song in perfect unison but the singer calls them 'fuckin' comedians' and 'cunts.' And then he reaches behind the guitarist and de-tunes his instrument."

"Oh god."

"Yeah. So then... Hunh. Oh, the singer, he sounds like a hurt animal and the band is paying him no mind. He starts noodling around on the woman's keyboards... until she turns it off. Oh, so then, the bass player and the guitar player and the drummer, they wave and walk off. The singer starts to prowl around, helping himself to whatever equipment he can scavenge. He fidgets with the knobs of the guitarist's amp, then he gives up and picks up the bass. He holds it a while, then throws the instrument across the stage. It goes over the drums and into the back wall."

"Wow."

"Yeah."

"I just don't get it. I thought... I thought what I shared with The Fall was this passion for ideas, for stories."

"I know. It's okay."

"The first time I heard them," Lady remembered, as the lightning came less frequently but thick rain escalated. "Well, I had a thing about Iceland, a place mad with literacy. Strong women. Hot springs. All my loves. A certain pupil of mine, Eloine Bowdonne—she had the loveliest hair, like corn-silk—she made me a cassette of Iceland-related material, songs by The Sugarcubes, that sort of affair. There was this thing on it called 'Iceland,' a very moody piece, very long. Conveying all the gloom, because, you know, it's often dark in Iceland, and the suspense, because people often drink there, and behave irrationally. Not that I've ever actually been there. Yet. But 'Iceland' was exactly how I'd imagined Iceland would sound. Something whistled in the background. Like a snatch of a farmer's radio. And the singer muttered. The band pleasantly went in and out."

"So that was the Fall?"

"Yeah."

A fleet of cement-mixers cruised past. One was playing swing music so loud the sidewalk shook.

"So how did..."

"Oh, so anyway, things with that pupil didn't work out so well, unfortunately. Her final paper for my class got lost. She claimed... well, it was preposterous." Ms Bowdonne said she placed it in the wrong mailbox in the faculty office of the Department of English on the last day of the semester. Never receiving it, Lady had been obligated to assign Ms Bowdonne a failing grade.

Lady heaved an enormous sigh. "So I kept up a bit with The Fall since those days. I'd go into the rock sections of HMV and hold all The Fall CDs, you know. I'd look at them. Sometimes I'd even buy one. I mean, it became clear that The Fall was drifting further from 'Iceland,' rather than nearer, I knew that. But still, I felt a kinship, a loyalty. It was just the music that made the most sense. It had all those literary references."

"I know."

Inside the club, Smith grasped yet another microphone in his hand. "Better listen to me," he was saying.

"Mark E!" Camden shouted.

There was an odd pause, prompting an audience member to ask, "Where are the words?"

"Words," Smith answered, "are the greatest expression. Of the Earth's... soul. As the *New York*

Times said. Yesterday. Our incorporation with musicians… "

He trailed off until Nagle's drum machine stopped playing.

"You better listen, 'cause town is a powderkeg. Radiohead. Radioactive force. I had a dream, one two three. Radiohead active. Where buck grunts had a program on the late TV."

The house lights came up. Taped music began to play on the overhead sound system.

"Turn the music off," Camden, along with many others, shouted.

"And then," Smith continued, "there's *three people* who had to *turn up* — and then… There was buck grunts. Three comedians. Then the owner of the Brownie's club was real glad to see the three comedians turn up. But what he didn't realize was… THIS TOWN IS A POWDERKEG! These three comedians, these buck grunts, didn't always have somebody else to live," he laughed to himself, "the next one. In combination. And the owner of the Brownie's club… just hopes… it made… three figures."

People laughed, applauded.

"Mark E!"

"See you," he mumbled. Smith walked off, hitting the keyboard on the way out. Nagle followed him.

At the bar, Fredericks and Hopper were suddenly jarred from their distracted observation of this strange performance. They did not know that, for the last half-hour, a primitive power had trapped them in its spell. They only grasped the danger of having allowed their attentions to stray. They pushed about the club in a slow-motion panic while the great majority of people moved against them, trying to leave.

The two men descended together upon the corridor outside the bathroom.

"What just happened here?" They looked anxiously from Vaughn to Colin and then back again. "Oh, Vaughn. Did someone get through the cage to you? You didn't give them the head, did you? Tell me they didn't enter your cage!"

Vaughn said nothing.

"Goodness!" shouted Fredericks.

"Oh no," said Hopper, "you don't know what this means. This is wretched."

Vaughn appeared entirely at ease. "Helen told me."

"Ah, Vaughn. I don't know what they told you. Whoever it was, *her name's not Helen*. She's a continuum pirate. *We're QST officers!*"

"Shit!" cried Colin, intuiting the disaster. He hurriedly kicked open the men's room door. The sink was now empty. "Shit!"

"This is truly terrible news for all of us, Vaughn," Hopper groaned. "Goodness!"

"Us?" Vaughn shook his head. "No."

They watched helplessly as Vaughn wended his

way through the crowd to join the others spilling from Brownie's. Everyone was careful not to bump into the two women who stood hugging in the downpour.

"Why do you like this band?" Vaughn heard one woman ask another, while steering her way around Betsy and Lady. "There is nothing great or honorable or even commendable about them… "

Many who were departing Brownie's merely congregated in clumps under the awning, caught unaware by the sudden thundershower. Brandon was on his cell-phone, paging Clarke to find out where in the hell he'd fled. Others stood and compared notes and shared disgruntlement.

"It was actually not horrifyingly violent," one man was saying.

"Well, what's your capsule review?"

"My capsule review? Let's see. The Fall fights like girlies, bickers, plays extraordinarily badly, plays extraordinarily well."

"And then some."

"I was just marveling," another spoke up while searching his coat for an umbrella, "marveling in its astonishingness."

An extremely thin redhead exited Brownie's just then, hollering at her group of extremely thin friends, "DON'T YOU EVER GET ME TO GO AND SEE A BAND LIKE THAT AGAIN!"

"I don't follow you," the short guy was conversing with the ROTC cadet, "you mean 'buck grunts' is army slang?"

"Yeah. A grunt is a private. 'Buck' means raw. Inexperienced."

"But one of those buck grunts has been in The Fall for twenty years!"

"Don't you think he meant the guitarist, though?"

Through it all, Betsy and Lady Millhauser hugged... though soon enough—they couldn't help it—they were giggling.

"Well," said Betsy. "It seems we're no longer so alone."

"No," said Lady.

"Listen... Do you want to get something?"

"Like dry clothes?"

"Umm... a drink?"

"Coffee?"

"Sure. Great. Coffee's great."

"I'd love that."

Inside, Tommy Crooks and Steve Hanley emerged from the back of Brownie's, intent on retrieving their stuff from the stage. Hanley looked about wildly, unable to tell where his bass had gone.

"Steve!" Tommy shouted over to him. "Steve, it's behind the drums."

Hanley fetched it, shaking his head. This whole tour had been so horribly unreal he could only apprehend it as the cumulative disaster in an MES bio-pic. He leaned in toward the clean-cut lad and his slender date. "Who's gonna play me in the movie?" Hanley laughed. He rose, then thought of someone. "—Sting!" He nodded, as if this fate was the horrible one he deserved. "Sting."

Tommy withdrew a disposable camera and snapped three flash pictures of the departing crowd. To a great ovation, he raised both arms, beaming, and strolled off.

THROUGH THE BRIGHTENING DAWN Vaughn walked everywhere weeping, he walked everywhere weeping, thinking how the vanished one he loved left him exposed like Band-Aids in a shower—he was weeping outside the stores where the deals get made and weeping in the streets where bargains get shouted (though none shouted at him)—tears beading on the arms and shoulders as though on a bench-presser's, skin bled sorrow, drenching the blouse in feelingful sobs, face contorted with grief: he could not find his feet, he sought to give the world words (to explain his weeping) which would not be, he could not, eyes and cheeks swollen, capillaries crimson with costly woe, he tried to regain composure again, again in vain, he went everywhere weeping, bumping and tripping and barely escaping while weeping this dawn he walked everywhere weeping wondering where he got turned around, all was

said and done in a moment in which he had
absented himself and in fact meant not only none
of it but nothing and did not weigh the weight of
lonely forevers (nor thinking of weeping this way)
today he walked everywhere, everywhere,
everywhere weeping: O Helen will I find you in
the errand-mothers, the lunch-break employees at
Radio City Station, the hapless ones pushing
squalling strollers, the knitcap hipsters, the techno
gals in floor-length flares and ball caps with bent-
down brims, the bill-payers in grimy workboots,
the women dragging roller-carts of items wrapped
in plastic bags... while babies cried and walkmans
played through the brightening dawn he walked
everywhere weeping, Charlie Brown kicking at a
just-moved football, thinking such sad things as
these had never before been seen, no nights so
black, through dawn he walked everywhere,
Herald Square to Prospect Park, broken painted
plates in shop windows sold for anything they'll
fetch, the air dense with storms of saccharine so
thick the flavoring settled deep in his fabric, he
lifted his hat and cheap sugars poured forth, it
caked upon his face where the tears took the
faked taste of sweetness to his tongue, weeping for
hostages overcome, postal workers come and
gone, innocent pails of water left out to rust, the
way the kids call each other, the people walking
alone — nothing sadder, nothing sadder — weeping
for those delicious hours spent awaiting the

repairmen of his youth, the man who lit their pilot light, the man who read the meter, the man who tapped their plumbing pipes with a mighty wrench—the man who'll fix his mother's washing machine! set the vcr! heal the microwave! explain to them the dishwasher!—oh men, you uncelebrated greats, drivers of company vans, wearers of tool belts, shivering the spine with your decisive diagnoses, your simple needs ("one glass of water coming right up!"), your extraordinary uses for everyday objects, your grip on the power of a crucial pause, your curative roving, leaving him inept to do a thing but wait for help, and wait for her and walk and wait, walk and wait, through dawn he walked everywhere waiting and weeping, taking the absence of everything as the sign of an imminent end, false walls, hollow sidewalks, weight-bearing loads, and him, separated from Helen by a distance unknowable. He wished to jump at the blimp and accuse it of ridiculous things, to push the moon into the earth's penumbra to assure himself of a lasting metaphor, this he thought through the dawn, as he walked utterly everywhere weeping, his heart a peeled-up can of oily sardines with the key gone, weeping for Helen...

Through the brightening dawn, Brandon sat in the back of his company car, parked in the garage, as he awaited the return of his chauffeur. Clarke awoke on the toilet of Brownie's with an ingenious plan to blackmail his way up the ladder at Seagram's through cognizance and resonance as Snook drew the curtains closed in his apartment and submerged himself in new calculations. Camden continued in his unkind ways, hacking into Snook's website at a random internet café to make sure that every mention of "The Fall" was followed by the parenthetical, "(who are a fucking GIMMICK)." Lady Millhauser peered from a bed in a midtown hotel and screeched, "Look at the time!" while the grinning Betsy ignored her, choosing instead to bask in rosy afterglow. In another hotel room, Mark E Smith was being arrested by officers responding to calls of a white female being choked, punched, and kicked (The Fall's keyboardist bore bruises and abrasions on her face, arms, and legs). Hearing the news, Sassy and Pat dissolved into pools of tears and Ken apologized profusely and the real-life golfing superhero, upon whom Colin's brother Robert B Morton based Matt Masters, rushed to the galactic aid of Phil's *Swamp Thing* to fight against the regenerated Pan for the liberation of all quantum space-time continuums and soon after—as Sweet Alicia's Necromicon begrudgingly foretold—they succeeded in their noble mission of good (though not without occasional consequent heartbreak on the part of them hapless mortals).

Through the brightening dawn, Colin moped

about Tompkins Square Park, looking for a place to rest. He settled presently upon a remote bench. The only others awake at this hour seemed to be bike cops, who periodically whirred past, casting him puzzled glances. He fell back but could not sleep; he could not stop obsessing about how pissed his Dad would be when he told him that he'd done exactly what he wasn't supposed to do. He had surrendered Pan to another continuum.

All at once, a female voice beside him whispered, "Spring is here."

Colin grunted, and shifted slightly away. He draped an arm over his eyes and tried, with his posture, to put forth the recommendation that he best be left alone.

"Listen," the woman kept on, in a somewhat sultry tone, "will you tell me something?"

At last, Colin lowered his arm to look at the woman. *Yes,* he thought groggily, *yes, I knew I recognized that voice.*

Drew Barrymore perched on a nearby bench, smiling sweetly. "Tell me how your parents support themselves."

Colin felt tears welling up in his eyes.

AS MORNING BROKE, Vaughn staggered exhaustedly up to his apartment building. He pushed into the vestibule and instinctively checked his mailbox.

There had been, of course, no post delivery since the previous evening. Still, it was his reflex to turn the key in the box and bend to look. Strangely, there was something: a small card, addressed to "Occupant" from "The National Center of Missing Citizens." He extracted it. Unlike the others he'd received, this one did not say, have you seen me. Instead it said, we found one. Frowning, Vaughn turned over the card. Beneath the usual date of birth there was no date of disappearance, but rather a date and location of discovery. He raised his eyes slightly to look at the picture.

It was Helen.

"Trust the Welsh to cause trouble."

— *Melody Maker*, 1993

1. **Fall, The.** A band from the north of England initially consisting of Mark E Smith, Una Baines, Karl Burns, Martin Bramah, and Tony Friel. This definition, however, has demanded a close and constant revision. When Mark E Smith is present, entity named The Fall is usually, but not always, present. When entity called The Fall is present, Mark E Smith is not always present. During only its first two years, Yvonne Pawlett replaced Una Baines, Mike Leigh replaced Karl Burns, Marc Riley replaced Tony Friel, then Riley replaced Martin Bramah when Steve Hanley joined, and then Riley replaced Pawlett when Craig Scanlon joined. With each new release, The Fall itself is new. These incessant redefinitions, in a way, define The Fall.

WELCOME READER NUMBER **000008**!

The first axiom states: if the lead singer is always not Mark E Smith, then entity is always not The Fall. This axiom is supported by two corollaries.

Corollary #1 draws upon "Favourite Sister" by Marc Riley and The Creepers. Riley had split from The Fall in 1982, after his renowned zaniness had invited Mark E Smith's ire (as relayed in the Creepers song, "Jumper Clown"). The split was acknowledged to've been acrimonious; in fact, French tabloids alleged "Marc et Mark" went mano a mano in a feisty tête-à-tête. Soon thereafter in record stores appeared "Favourite Sister," which featured every Fall member except Mark E Smith. Some would ask, was this The Fall? No. With Marc Riley always the lead singer, then The Creepers was always not The Fall.

Corollary #2 recounts how, in the sticky June of 1985, recordings emerged from a band consisting entirely of Fall members with Mrs. Mark E Smith on vocals and her husband in clandestine production mode. Some would ask, was this The Creepers then, or The Fall? Neither. The group was Adult Net, still another entity.

In full confidence, one can even assert the following: if entity is always The Fall, then lead singer is not always Mark E Smith. The proof of this relies upon the oft-ignored fact that The Fall was formed, in early 1977, with Martin Bramah as the lead singer. At the time, Mark E Smith was solely employed to ornament their songs by picking at a guitar in a most unusually spiderish manner. Additionally, there are many possible configurations in which The Fall could remain The Fall without Mark E Smith. Just to put the cat amongst the pigeons, I cite the following examples:

   i. Getting rid of the main guy in the group who'd had all the ideas and keeping the name he'd thunk up (e.g., Pink Floyd)

   ii. The main guy in the group getting rid of the rest of them, keeping the name he'd thunk up, for a bit (e.g., The Mothers of Invention) (NB, in this case the band was together under a different name before the main guy came along)

   iii. Getting rid of everyone who has ever been in the group and replacing them with other people, some of whom have even been together in other groups (e.g., Soft Machine)

iv. Getting rid of band, replacing them with session musicians doing MOR crap for a bit, and keeping name (Captain Beefheart and The Magic Band) whilst band goes off and replaces singer with some c&w guy (Mallard)

v. All the original members having departed, the guitarist, who only joined in time for the third album, retains the names, ropes in Deep Purple's drummer, and then shamelessly releases another album with no credits whatsoever in the forlorn hope that people might be dumb enough to fall for this ruse (The Velvet Underground's fifth studio album, *Squeeze*)

vi. The iconic outspoken poet and all-round genius having stomped off in disgust, the band replaces him with a moronic criminal before making a poxy movie accusing said genius of being a "collaborator" (Sex Pistols)

This actually conforms to the rule of When Ruben And The Jets Is Not The Mothers Of Invention ("when Motorhead Sherwood Is Present, entity is still Ruben And The Jets"). Only The Residents, Schroedinger's Cat-like, defy it.

THERE HAVE BEEN `000008`

HITS ON THIS PAGE!

Click **here** for rates if you wish to book Alvin Snook as your party entertainment.

2. **The Fall – *Levitate* (Artful, UK Import)**. There's a feeling of renewed confidence here. Perhaps having finally adjusted to the loss of principle guitarist Craig Scanlon, the band offer the least guitar-based (keyboardist Julia Nagle makes a major contribution) and most noise-oriented Fall album. They've finally figured out just what

to do with their Krautrock influences. This is the first Fall album on which MES is solely responsible for production, and he does a pleasingly varied job. The unadorned, dry production of "Ten Houses" contrasts nicely with the scratty psychedelics that turn up later on "Hurricane Edward" and "Ol' Gang." There's a most ingenious, self-deprecating (I hope) cover of '50's novelty number "I'm a Mummy," and a most un-Fall-like, not-quite-like-anything-you've-heard-before instrumental called "Jap Kid." "I Come and Stand at Your Door" is "Jap Kid" with vocals, and sounds like a Frank Sinatra song from *The Man with the Golden Arm* if that movie had songs. There's the obligatory pointless lo-fi track that sounds like (and probably is) someone mucking about at home on a tape machine; this time it's called "Tragic Days."

3. **The Fall – *Chaos 006* (Chaos Tapes).** The Fall have always reveled in being a sloppy bunch, and their unashamed, workman-like determination to persevere through bad situations opens them up to glorious accidents, leakages of spontaneous genius. The best evidence is the cassette Chaos 006, documenting The Fall at Acklam Hall in London 1980, performing as a band at odds with everything—its own members and instruments and material, its audience, its culture. Songs cues are botched, lyrics dropped, harmonies sabotaged, strings broken. "[If] we were smart," MES concedes at one point, "we'd emigrate." For the first time, the audience claps in encouragement. Compared to The Fall, the rest of the music world weighs in as unbearably straight.

Murky and mean to the ear, *Chaos 006* is my favorite release from the early 1980's. My copy is No. 2001 from a limited edition of 4000. I've owned it over fifteen years. Its producer, Chaos Tapes, appears not to be a real entity; it may've produced bootlegs. In place of a record company address, there is, on the sleeve, a note: "No correspondence can be entered into – sorry." I can't remember where I got it. When I bought it, the tape already wobbled; I came to adore its poor quality.

Recalled on *Chaos 006* are the oft-unrecalled days when Kay Carroll managed and Marc Riley guitared, before The Fall received proper promotion/distribution from Beggars Banquet (1984), when good production values were still too expensive, before Brix descended to Yoko-ize the situation.

Just over three years old, The Fall in 1980 had already undergone nine switches in personnel and four changes in label. The Fall was now indisputably MES's if merely because he was the only founding member who'd survived all the putsches and purges. Considering this persistent upheaval, The Fall's output was astonishing: they averaged two new albums (plus two non-album 45s) every year from 1978 to 1984, an unending torrent of pun-filled mysteries involved inspectors and specters and rectors, short stories of recursive time-loops, city hobgoblins, inflamed characterizations, livid generalizations, nerve storms, untuned instruments, and bumped mikes, which, upon repeated listenings, came off so surely as brilliant.

Somewhere on every one of those albums Mark E Smith used at least one song to brag about his band – The Fall, whose record this was – and such jubilant self-involvement rang with a genuine, if short-sighted, charisma – one of the many ways in which The Fall presaged rap music. Rap finally answered Mark E Smith's challenge that "nobody tells stories anymore, nobody uses loud amplifiers. It's all down on paper now." Rap came in when The Fall began to grow dull, around 1982, and made irrelevant most of what The Fall did – the throwing of too many syllables into songs, the placing of words in songs with attention purely to their rhythms. Thereafter only Mark E Smith's voice remained unique, that impenetrable Mancunian accent, thrown uncommonly into the microphone, frightening studio engineers with random mumbles and shrieks.

Hearing Mark E Smith on *Chaos 006*, one gets the sense of a criminal goading an attacking audience. You wait for the crowd to overwhelm him though what he's chanting at them in his flat rancid voice is usually abstract diatribes. He's a blind-drunk policy wonk about to lose his life, chuckling at his own clever asides. The music is very secondary.

The fact that Mark E Smith spent his boyhood taking psychedelics while hanging with the math nerds in his school always seemed the most relevant anecdote when commenting upon The Fall. After all, when done right, music (insist people who know a lot more about music than I do) *is* mathematics; but even after growing up, Mark E Smith remained estranged from such mechanistic analyses (apart though awkwardly near), using academic sources as he used every source—ham radio, junk mail, football disputes, misspelled graffiti—as something which was eager to be turned into nonsense.

Not so much anymore do Mark E Smith's wrath and rancor sound a wartime clarion, perhaps because no Fall thing feels so handmade anymore, between the lovely jackets (worn both by the band and its releases) and the attentively produced, well-mixed tracks (more like conventional songs now than ever before). Nobody turns on the television in the middle of doing vocals anymore and they apparently do several takes now rather than extemporizing without rehearsals.

4. **Do I Dare to Fireball Atomic?** Last night I dreamt 1979. The ZERRIN-17s — the enemy's big yellows — rumbled through the villages. Again we ran giggling around the camps, finding it hysterical that our living quarters were all identical, rejoicing how none of us had mothers or fathers anymore.

The enemy, having just arrived, were stupid. They believed we were children such as they had experienced, gay and frivolous. We were not. They courteously stooped to inquire directions and we pointed them into ambushes. Winking, they tossed us coins and we tossed them booby-trapped necklaces that bore bombs where their "Capt. Zerrin" buttons belonged. They happily accepted the gifts we bestowed, the gasoline we assured them was our finest liquor, the blocks of poison we called "gourmet hashish," and one by one they toasted us in merry celebration, then died. Most of the enemy were only five or six years older but something made it inarguable to us that they'd grown up to be expendable. Their trust of us came to be short-lived. Within the year, kids were treated as dependents of the friends to the enemies of the people; most were shot on sight.

Thereafter I cowered in a clock-infested cellar where I tended timepieces, winding them till my wrists grew heavy, crossing out the days until these invaders would break camp in panic. Interference from the ammunition dump blew out my radio connection to Headquarters. Against the damn eternal tick-tick-tock-tick I played The Fall's *Dragnet* (Step Forward SFLP4), which one of the fleeing Embassy brats had left cued up on his reel-to-reel. The abandoned spool of shined brown Ampex unwound for me like an entrancing ritual, the tool of a seance, moving to the pick-up reel across the hypnotized heads of the Tascam 32. *Dragnet* stank of bad breath, primitives wrestling with the supernatural. "His friends are full of evil serum," went one murder song. "The streets are full of mercenary eyes." It sounded to be recorded using soup cans and string, in the days before color was invented. What those spoilt diplomatic children made of such crudeness was anybody's guess, when their own skin was so soft you could cut it with a butter knife. It was an album one of their espionage dads perhaps surreptitiously picked up through a fuzzy government wiretap.

I burrowed deeper amongst the clocks, lived on The Fall and a cache of spicy American jawbreakers called Atomic Fireballs. I changed my all-okay from the sentry to, "Do I dare to fireball atomic?"

I broke out in sweats consuming these rationed wartime candies, tearing up as they stung the tongue and bloodied the mouth with red dye, while howitzers pounded, maintenance depots blew, agents bungled against trip-wires, civilian bodies burned, clocks ticked, and the lead singer of The Fall droned, "Onto the scene now comes a hero. This hero was a strange man. 'Those flowers, take them away,' he said. 'They're only funeral decorations. I know: this is a drudge nation; a nation of no imagination. The stupid dead man is their ideal.'" The singer bore this anonymous name: Mark E Smith.

Love songs sounded absurd in the clock cellar. Melodies were lies. Hearing some pop humanitarian would have nauseated me; much more I sought the confused rantings of some zealous comrade. *Dragnet* supplied that, conveying the drama of Mark E Smith's overpowering indifference. He may've hated music, for he sounded dim of generosity and quick to judge, but still his music could not be turned off. And every talent, Nietzsche said, must unfold itself in fighting—and yeah, had grand Germany's scornful genius led "ein band der rocken roll" it would doubtless have been Das Fall.

The stuff didn't promote good neighborly relations, didn't bother with a humanist set-up, it was about dictatorship, pure and simple. So what? Do we put on this stuff in order to form a more perfect union?

Many are the fingers pointed now that point out we couldn't govern worth a damn once we regained power because our generation lacked democratic role models and because, as for myself, I knew only The Fall. This morning I awoke to the same old headaches, the disparaging dispatches from the know-nothing press corps. It's hard enough to learn how to kill and how to love, and next to advance that in some sort of diplomatic dialogue—but to ask us to then make sure our taste comfortably adheres to some particular ideology of universal values, as we navigate our emotional journeys by pop stars, how can this be? Either we are honest to ourselves or we are good citizens, but so often aren't these mutually exclusive?

5. Matt Masters was just a fair-to-middling professional golfer until clubs from outer-space were bequeathed him by the Guardians of the Universe, on condition that he, as the Golden Golfer, fight for Truth, Justice, and—that ubiquitous sweeping constant—the American Way. Masters was abducted to a Pacific Island where a warrior who didn't know that the 16th Century had ended taught him samurai golfing techniques. The clubs required a lot of unlikely coincidences to operate as weapons. Suffice it to say that Matt Masters patrolled the streets of New York fighting crime by ricocheting golfballs off buildings in a fashion which the Guardians had always denied the English (and also, due to a loss in translation, the Welsh).

6. **From "Neighborhood of Infinity," The Homepage of Alvin Snook.** Using The Rule Of Soft Machine ("when no members of Soft Machine are present entity is still Soft Machine") with a flourish ("even if all members of nucleus are present") one can prove that Entity known as The Fall exists even when No Members Of The Fall Are Present.

After The Fall lost its English-speaking members, it picked up temporary members around the globe to assert a continued presence.

...The Fall manifested itself during the snake slaughter's four days of dancing and singing in Nepal. Chariots raced in the narrow streets. The upper and lower parts of Bhaktapur engaged in their annual game of tug of war to decide who would be fortunate in the coming year. A Tibetan troupe, associated with the innovative Blue Masked Sect, evoked an immediate mood or imagery in a simple language, employing both metaphor and hidden analogy, their harmonies broken in the manner of Tibetan opera. Suddenly one voice amongst them was heard to holler: *stupa chorten kunzang khorlo chosi nyiden bindu auyoga tib tashi tagye* (loosely, "we are that most honorable white detritus from the North that may be said to speak back").

The Fall was also experienced by many on the Song Huon Floating Restaurant in Vietnam's central provinces. American war enthusiasts had paid 15,000 us dollars apiece to fly to Hue and take part in the bone-chilling re-enactment of 1968's bitter house-to-house combat, along with the more famous moments of that February's counter-assault which dislodged nva forces from the citadel. Afterwards, the Americans celebrated with fermented spices, drifting on sampans down the well-mosquitoed Perfume River and hearing performances of the traditional Ca Hue folk songs. The instruments were wooden, garnished with old coins. Four bone-china coffee cups provided the percussion section. The lyrics eulogized the city's beautiful scenery or the ten charms of a Hue woman — including her long hair, dreamy eyes, flowing *ao dai*, and conical hat — until a shift in delivery and lyrical emphasis took place. "There's a party going on down here," exploded a harsh voice, which witnesses later compared to a howitzer. "On Cruiser's Creek, yeah."

A small amount of time later, during a cabaret act in the central square of Jendouba in Tunisia, a belly dancer turned her back to the audience in the patented style of Mark E Smith and embarked upon a long narrative prose-poem that spoke of how, "The north will rise again." Even more alarming was her absurd use of kazoo during the recitation. State authorities were caught utterly by surprise and could take no action. In defense, they pointed out that the only remarkable thing in Jendouba previously had been the collection of storks' nests on the roofs of the central square.

Soon after, the spirit of The Fall descended upon a tiny tract of disputed territory within what is currently Jordan. There, during a performance of hypnotic music, a medium entered a ritualistic trance state. She became possessed by a seemingly British deity, chanting, "I'm totally wired. T-t-t-totally wired. And I'm always worried." These rhythmic ceremonies are instrumental in goddess worship. Because of the government's anti-religious stance, this ancient, sacred style is practiced in secret…

These are just four examples extracted from the full report. The list goes on and on.

For their assistance, the authors wish to thank the following Mark Smiths:

Mark Lerner Smith
Mark Steve Smith
Mark Rimell Smith
Mark Devlin Smith
Mark Czekaj Smith
Mark John Williams Smith
Mark Kaminker Smith
Mark Summers Smith
Mark Good Ben Smith
and Mark Robert B Morton Smith.

COLOPHON

This book is set in Linotype Didot, a typeface drawn by Adrian Frutiger in 1991 and based on fonts cut in Paris by Firmin Didot between 1799 and 1811. The original Didot types defined the characteristics of the modern (or Didone) roman type style.

The book was designed by Mark Lerner at Rag & Bone Shop in New York City and printed by Westcan Printing Group in Winnipeg. Title page calligraphy is by Nancy Howell.